Danger Marches to the Palace

Queen Lili'uokalani

by Margo Sorenson

Cover Photo: The Granger Collection
Inside Illustration: Dea Marks

For Jim, Jane, and Jill, my wonderful family, who share my aloha for this land.
For Lucy, cheerleader, horizon-expander, and Islands fan extraordinaire.

About the Author

Margo Sorenson was born in Washington, D.C. She spent the first seven years of her life in Europe, living where there were few children her age. She found books to be her best friends and read constantly. Ms. Sorenson wrote her own stories too. Her first one was called "Leo and Bo-Peep," which still makes her laugh today.

Ms. Sorenson finished her school years in California, graduating from the University of California at Los Angeles. She taught high school and middle school and raised a family of two daughters. Ms. Sorenson is now a full-time writer, writing primarily for young people junior high age or older. Ms. Sorenson enjoys writing for these age groups since she believes they are ready for new ideas and experiences, and they really enjoy "living" the lives of the characters in books.

After having lived in Hawaii and California, Ms. Sorenson now lives in Minnesota with her husband. She enjoys traveling to Europe and visiting places she might write about. When she isn't writing, she enjoys reading, sports, and traveling.

Text © 1998 by Perfection Learning® Corporation.

Printed in the United States of America. For information, contact
Perfection Learning® Corporation, Logan, Iowa 51546-1099.
Paperback ISBN 0-7891-2154-9
Cover Craft® ISBN 07-807-6788-8

Contents

1

Lost in the Jungle

"I do *not*," Aleesa snapped. "I swear! You get on my nerves!" She made a face at Kenneth. Then she slumped down in the bus seat.

Next to Aleesa, Kenneth shook his head. He stared out the bus window. Shouts, laughter, and joking filled the inside of the bus.

"Carissa! You can't do *that!*"

"Look, Aadeel. Look out the window!"

"Bradley, come sit over here!"

The rest of the science class was having a great time. Everyone was excited. Everyone but him. Kenneth frowned. He had Aleesa for a science partner. Great. A science field trip and who did *he* have? Aleesa again.

And they were stuck as partners for the dumb social studies project too. He looked up for a second. Did somebody have it in for him, or what?

"All right, class," Ms. Harper announced. She stood by the bus driver, holding on to the chrome pole.

The bus engine roared. The driver shifted gears. The gears ground. The bus pulled out of the Berkeley Middle School lot. Ms. Harper swayed. She caught her balance. Aleesa grinned. That'd be pretty funny, wouldn't it? If Harper landed flat on her behind in the bus? She smothered a giggle.

Kenneth looked over at her. What was she snickering about now? He just couldn't figure Aleesa out.

"All right, class," Ms. Harper repeated patiently. "Please be quiet." She waited while the noise stopped. A giggle here. A whisper there. Finally, only the sound of the bus engine filled the air.

Aleesa sighed. She looked at Ms. Harper. Boring, boring. Here we go, she thought.

"At the Berkeley Arboretum, we're going to study some plants," Ms. Harper said. Her voice droned on and on.

Aleesa closed her eyes. Maybe she could pretend she was on some tropical island somewhere. Far, far away from dumb school and dumb projects. Not to mention dumb Kenneth.

Kenneth tapped his fingers on the window ledge. Maybe he could pretend he was on a beach somewhere. Some place where Aleesa *wasn't*. Sometimes it seemed as if the teachers had planned it all out. Teachers loved to torture students, didn't they? They kept putting Aleesa and Kenneth together on projects. And social studies would be the worst. He frowned. "You'll work together on this. So you can balance each other out," Ms. Carter said in social studies yesterday. Her smile stopped just below her eyes. "Aleesa, you have energy. Kenneth, you are a planner. Your native rights project will be good, I'm sure."

Right, Kenneth snorted to himself, thinking back over yesterday. Native rights. Who cared? And Aleesa had energy all right. She was just crazy, that was all. She kept jumping into stuff without thinking. He sighed. But they were stuck together. He had to try to make the best of it. He needed a good grade on the native rights project. After all, he had to keep his grades up for football.

"All right," Kenneth said. He turned to Aleesa. "Have you thought about what old Carter told us? About our social studies project? Or did you already forget?"

She rolled her eyes up to the bus ceiling. What lecture was Kenneth going to give her now? He thought he knew everything.

"Okay, you do *not* forget everything." He grinned wickedly. "At least—you don't forget when the mall closes." He laughed at his own joke.

Aleesa stuck her tongue out at Kenneth. Then she looked serious.

"Look," she challenged. "Do you want to get going on this project, or not?" she asked. "Then quit hassling me." She folded her arms. She stared straight ahead in the bus.

"Okay, okay," Kenneth said, still grinning. "Chill, will you? So, which native rights group do you want to do? Inuits in Alaska? Hawaiians in Hawaii? Native Americans?"

Tropical island, Aleesa thought again. "Let's do the Hawaiians," she said. "Maybe you can give your part of the report in a hula skirt." She dissolved into giggles.

"Very funny," Kenneth said. He frowned. The guys on the football team would love that.

"Okay. Fine. The native Hawaiians. But they lived in grass huts, right? They didn't care if they became part of the U.S. After all, they had a queen or something. Imagine. That's pretty old-fashioned. It was better for them to be in the U.S., don't you think?" he asked.

"Uh-uh. This is one part of the chapter I really read," Aleesa taunted him. She stuck her tongue out at him again. "There was some revolution—or something." She crinkled her forehead. What had the chapter said, exactly? Now she couldn't remember. Uh-oh. "Well, anyway, the Hawaiians weren't too happy. You'll find out," she said quickly. And so would she. As soon as she had a chance to look in the textbook again. Kenneth better not find out that she couldn't remember.

Aleesa was full of baloney, Kenneth thought. Hah. He just *bet* she read the chapter. Right. When pigs had wings.

"Here we are, class," Ms. Harper announced. She stood up. The bus lurched and slowed down. Ms. Harper grabbed the pole. She stayed upright.

Darn, Aleesa thought. Ms. Harper's balance was better than she thought. Ms. Harper falling splat on the floor of the bus would have made her day. Aleesa sighed. She looked out the window.

A big green sign next to the road welcomed them. "Berkeley Arboretum" it read. A gate guard waved them through. Its brakes huffing, the bus jerked to a stop next to a low building.

"Now go with your partners," Ms. Harper was saying. "Identify the plants on the sheet. Listen carefully to our guide. And stay together," she added. "I don't want anyone to get lost. I don't want to have to rescue you."

Everyone pushed and shoved to get off the bus. Aleesa followed Kenneth. Kids moved out of his way. Huh. That's one thing he was good for, she thought. He could break a path for her. Guess football helped after all.

Now if only they didn't have to get a grade for this stupid field trip. Grandma would put her in a closet until she was thirty if she got one more lousy grade. And then there would be a grade for the social studies project too. She frowned. She had it rough. No kidding.

Aleesa looked ahead at the towering trees. Leafy branches spread everywhere. Bright flowers peeked out from jungly-looking plants. At least they weren't back at school. It would be kind of a nice walk. Too bad they had work to do. And too bad she had to be with Kenneth.

A whole two hours with Aleesa, Kenneth grumbled to himself. He stepped off the bus. He'd better really pay attention to the guide. Or they'd get a bad grade on this too. He shoved his hands into his pockets. Mom would really go ballistic if his grades went down. Football would be the first to go. And he had that social studies project on native rights. With Aleesa. He shook his head. That was a big-deal grade too. Trouble ahead, for sure.

"Stay together, boys and girls," a uniformed guide said. She motioned for them to come closer. "It's easy to get lost in here. The arboretum is many square acres of trees and plants."

"Boys and girls," Aleesa mimicked in a low voice to Kenneth. "How old does she think we are, anyway?" Aleesa put her shoulders back. She strutted forward. Kenneth followed with a sigh.

The guide led them down path after path. "These plants have all been donated. Many college and university students come here . . ." she went on. After a few more paths, "This is our tropical section." She stopped. She pointed to a palm tree. "This is a tree of the family *Palmaceae* . . ."

"Boring, boring, boring," Aleesa whispered to Kenneth. She stopped. Kenneth almost ran into her. There were some beautiful yellow flowers growing next to the path. "Look," she said. She kneeled down. "Look how pretty these are." She reached out and touched the yellow petals. They were almost silky to the touch.

Kenneth looked up. The guide and the class had gone ahead. They had disappeared around a bend. "Hey," he warned. "Let's catch up. I don't want to spend the night in here."

"You won't," Aleesa said. "They're right around the corner." She broke off one of the flowers. She smelled it. A thick perfume drifted around her. She shut her eyes. She could almost hear pounding surf and rustling palm trees. "This smells so pretty," she said. "Here," she added. She grinned and thrust the flower in Kenneth's face.

"Phew!" he exclaimed. "Flowers. Give me a break." He pushed the flower away. It had a heavy, sweet scent. It smelled like no flower he'd ever been around.

Aleesa still held the flower. The sound of rustling palm trees grew louder. The air grew warmer. She frowned. She looked at Kenneth. "Hey," she said. "Is something weird going on?"

Kenneth wiped the sweat from his forehead. He unzipped his jacket. "I don't know. It's awful warm all of a sudden, don't you think?" he asked. He looked around

11

them. Hadn't the sky gotten a brighter blue? His head reeled suddenly.

"I . . . I'm kinda dizzy," Aleesa mumbled. She dropped the flower. Reaching out to lean against a palm tree, she shut her eyes. "Maybe if I just rest a second," she said.

"I . . . I guess I will too," Kenneth said. He stared at the flower Aleesa had dropped. "Do . . . do you think it was poisonous?" he asked. He heard a ringing in his ears. He shut his eyes.

"Aaiiiee!" a voice squealed. Kenneth and Aleesa both opened their eyes.

Behind them stood a dark-skinned girl about their age. But she was dressed in some old costume. It was like the girl thought it was Halloween or something. She looked like she was back in the olden days. Long skirts, all that stuff. Weird place, this arboretum.

"What's up?" Kenneth managed to say. Weird chick, he thought. Looked like she got her clothes at some old-time thrift shop. Except they didn't look old—they looked brand new.

The girl backed up. She looked up, puzzled. "The palm tree branches are up," she said. "And the sky is up too," she added, looking back at Kenneth and Aleesa. "Are . . . are you new here?" She hid her trembling hands behind her back. "Are you here to serve Queen Lili'uokalani?"

"Queen *who?*" Kenneth croaked. Wait a second. Something was really off base around here. Was someone playing a joke on them? He looked around to see if any of his buddies from the football team were hiding nearby, laughing their heads off. Nope. Just a brightly-colored bird squawked on a branch.

The girl looked impatient. "The queen," she said. "Queen Lili'uokalani. The queen of Hawaii. Who else?"

"The queen of Hawaii?" Kenneth repeated in a daze. "Lili . . . whatever?"

"The queen?" Aleesa breathed. She pinched herself.

The girl looked them up and down. "Yes. You must be from Maui," she decided. "Your clothes look like it."

Kenneth stared down. His heart nearly stopped. Gone were his jeans and his shirt. No more Nikes on his feet. Instead he was wearing some weird old-time outfit.

He looked over at Aleesa. She was staring down at her clothes too. And she looked really different.

Aleesa couldn't believe her outfit. Her pulse raced. What in the world was she wearing? It looked like the girl's dress. It was long and really, really old-fashioned. What had happened?

Panicked, she and Kenneth stared at each other. Aleesa swallowed hard. Kenneth felt sweat bead on his forehead.

Where were they?

2

Bayonet Constitution

"I . . . I didn't know who you were, at first," the girl stammered. She took a few steps closer. "You . . . you can't be too careful these days," she warned softly.

What? Kenneth wondered. What was happening here? The girl looked around nervously. Kenneth looked too. No one was there.

He saw palm trees and flowers. A fancy iron fence surrounded them. Over the fence he could see a huge building. What was that? He didn't remember that at the arboretum.

"Why not? Why do you have to be careful?" Aleesa asked. She put her hands on her hips. What was happening, anyway? This sounded weird.

"I . . . I was afraid . . . at first," the girl confessed. "I heard rustling. I didn't know who it was. I was afraid it might be messengers for the Honolulu Rifles. Or the Annexation Club."

"The what Rifles?" Kenneth asked. He shook his head. Rifles? This didn't sound too good.

"The Honolulu Rifles," the girl answered. She looked puzzled. "You two really are just off the boat from Maui, aren't you? I thought everyone knew. The Honolulu Rifles forced the king to sign the Bayonet Constitution six years ago. They almost killed him."

She lowered her voice. Aleesa and Kenneth stepped closer to hear.

"And some of the Rifles' members started the Annexation Club eight months ago," she went on. "It's supposed to be a secret club. But everyone knows about it. We're sure the Annexation Club is planning something terrible." She shook her head. "The queen of Hawaii is in danger."

Wait a second. Hawaii? Kenneth stared at the girl. She said Hawaii again. A chill ran down Kenneth's spine.

She was serious. This wasn't any practical joke some guys on his football team were playing. What had happened to him and Aleesa?

He looked around again. Palm trees. Flowers. Ferns. So . . . it looked as if they really *were* in Hawaii. But . . . but why was she talking about a queen? Hawaii was part of the United States. There was no queen in the U.S.

Thoughts flashed through his head. Then he swallowed hard. It couldn't be. Were they back in time? Back to when Hawaii had been its own country? And a queen had ruled? He looked over at Aleesa. This was like that native rights stuff from social studies class. Were they going to be trapped in a revolution?

Aleesa's eyes were wide. She was staring at the girl in shock. She was stunned into silence. No! she thought. We're back in the 1800s? What were they going to do? How were they going to get back to their own time? she wondered.

They had to start getting some answers, Kenneth decided. What year was it? When was it the queen was overthrown, anyway? He winced. Too bad he hadn't read the whole chapter.

"Uh . . . what's your name?" he asked.

"Mary," she said. "Mary Puanani Hayes," she added. She held up the covered basket she was carrying. It had a royal crown painted on the side. "I'm in the queen's household too. An attendant. Just like you," she said.

Just like you? Aleesa almost choked. The queen's

household? Attendant? Did that mean she had to do stuff for the queen? Help! she wanted to yell.

Just like you? Kenneth repeated to himself. What did kids do in the queen's household? Was he going to wash her cars? Uh-uh—no cars, right? This had to be before cars. Maybe her *carriages?*

"I'm on an errand," Mary went on. "The queen is sending directions for making a feather *lei* to her good friend Mrs. Boyd. So I'm on my way to the Boyds'." Mary looked at them. "Do you want to come too?"

Aleesa looked at Kenneth. Now what? This was really strange. Her heart raced. It must be 1890-something. She squeezed her eyes shut. Why couldn't she remember the chapter?

Mary looked at them curiously. "Well? Do you want to come or not?" She waited. "And what are your names?" she asked.

"Uh . . . Aleesa," Aleesa said. "Aleesa Strong." She looked at Kenneth. Did she do the right thing by saying her real name?

"I'm Kenneth. Kenneth Smith," Kenneth said. Telling her his name was okay, wasn't it? Could that get them in more trouble?

"Hmmm," Mary said. She looked them up and down. Then she smiled. "Well, welcome, Kenneth and Aleesa. I heard the queen was getting some more attendants from Maui. I'm glad you're here. We could use the help," she said. She looked around again. "Especially these days.

17

Sometimes I get really afraid. Let's go," she said. She hurried down the path.

Kenneth and Aleesa fell into step with Mary. "What do you mean?" Kenneth asked. "Why are you afraid? Isn't it the queen who's in danger?"

He glanced at Aleesa. She looked back at him worriedly. His mouth tightened. A lot was happening here. Rifles? Bayonets? And Mary was afraid.

"You don't know much out on Maui, do you?" Mary said, teasingly.

Maui? Oh, yeah. One of those other islands. Hawaii always confused him. Too many islands. And all the names sounded alike.

"Uh, no," Kenneth said quickly. "So tell us," he said.

Aleesa followed Mary and Kenneth through a huge gate. They had been in a garden. She looked back over her shoulder. Behind the garden, she saw a huge, beautiful building with a tower in front.

The Hawaiian royal palace! Iolani Palace, wasn't it? It had to be. Her mouth felt dry. This was really happening. She shivered in spite of the heat.

"Why is the queen in danger?" Aleesa asked. She wished she could remember what the textbook said.

"Don't you remember? It started a long time ago. King Kalakaua, the queen's brother? He had to sign the horrible Bayonet Constitution," Mary said. "The terrible men in the Hawaiian League made the king sign it. The Honolulu Rifles helped them. The businessmen and foreigners were in on it. That was six years ago. 1887. And now the businessmen want even more power. They keep arguing with the queen."

1887? Kenneth's stomach tightened. Six years ago? Great. That meant now it was 1893. How would they ever get out of 1893?

"Of course," Aleesa said quickly. "The Bayonet Constitution." Well, she sort of remembered the chapter. Some businessmen and some Americans took power away from the king. That was about all she could remember.

Mary frowned. "It was just so unfair," she said, stepping across a dusty street. Kenneth and Aleesa followed.

"The foreigners and businessmen like the Bayonet Constitution," she sighed. "It took power away from a lot of us native Hawaiians. And the king too." She looked at Kenneth and Aleesa. "To vote, you don't even have to be a Hawaiian citizen. Some foreigners are citizens of Hawaii, of course. Some Americans and Germans and others have lived here a long time. They became Hawaiian citizens. That's all right for them to vote."

Mary stopped. She untied her bonnet. She swung it back and forth by the ribbon ties.

This sounded weird, Kenneth thought. Everyone in Hawaii today was a *U.S.* citizen. And they should be, he told himself. The U.S. is great.

Mary went on. "But a lot of native Hawaiians can't

vote now. The Bayonet Constitution says you have to be rich to vote. You have to own property. You need money. Can you believe it? We don't even get to govern ourselves any more. But the businessmen and foreigners made the king sign it. They threatened him with bayonets. Weren't your parents mad about that too?"

"Uh, yeah, sure," Kenneth mumbled. He looked at Aleesa. Don't say anything stupid, he begged silently.

"Uh-huh," Aleesa added. "My grandma was pretty mad." She smiled triumphantly. There, that was a touch of the truth. Grandma was usually pretty mad—mad at her!

"Your *tutu?*" Mary asked.

"Um . . . um . . . yes," Aleesa stammered. She saw Mary smile. Whew. She got lucky. *Tutu* must mean grandma in Hawaiian. Maybe she'd have to be more careful about what she said.

Kenneth held back a sigh. There went Aleesa again. Who knew what kind of trouble she could get them into here?

Aleesa looked at Kenneth. He was shaking his head at her. He always thought he was right. No matter what.

"But why is there trouble now? Why are you afraid?" Kenneth asked.

"Well," Mary said slowly. She lowered her voice. Kenneth and Aleesa crowded closer to her. "It's like I said. King Kalakaua died almost two years ago. But the foreigners—Americans mostly—have been trying to get even *more* power from the queen."

Mary looked around her again at the street. Kenneth looked too. No one paid attention to them. A carriage rattled past. But hardly anyone else was around, Kenneth noticed.

"The queen took over for her brother. But she's had nothing but trouble. We think the businessmen and foreigners want to get rid of the queen now," she said. "And those awful men in the Annexation Club—" Mary stopped. She took a deep breath. "They . . . they want the Kingdom of Hawaii to end. They want us to be part of the United States," she finished. "No more Hawaii," Mary said.

Her eyes looked really sad, Aleesa thought. Oh, my gosh, she realized. There really *would* be no more kingdom. Hawaii would become part of the U.S., for sure. It really would happen that way in history. Of course, Mary didn't know.

"Well, what's so bad about that?" Kenneth asked. "What's wrong with Hawaii becoming part of the U.S.?" This was just what he was trying to argue with Aleesa on the bus. That native Hawaiian rights stuff. He saw Aleesa dart a glance at him. Why did she look so upset?

"What?" Mary squeaked. "What is wrong with you? No more Kingdom of Hawaii? That's treason! You sound like a traitor! You don't really mean that, do you?"

Kenneth stared at Mary. Great. What had he done? It was something Aleesa would have done—yapped

21

without thinking.

"Uh . . . uh . . . no," Kenneth stammered. Just be quiet for a while, he told himself.

See? Aleesa wanted to snap back. He was going to get them into trouble, after all. She knew it. And he always told her that *she* was the one who opened her mouth. This time it was Kenneth. Hah.

Mary shook her head. "Think about it. Then we native Hawaiians will have no power at all," she said. "It's our land. Our country. The foreigners will run everything. Even now they take our land, our *aina*. They don't respect our customs. They don't care about our traditions. Don't you remember? The missionaries even stopped the hula. Until King Kalakaua made it all right again."

"The hula! You do the hula?" Aleesa exclaimed. Kenneth jabbed her with his elbow. She jumped. Then she made a face at him.

"And you know, our kings and queens really care about us Hawaiians." Mary gestured with her hand holding the basket. "Especially our queen." She smiled. "Queen Lili'uokalani is wonderful. She has traveled all over the world. Queen Victoria in England is her friend. The queen is kind. She is generous. And she wants us to have our rights back."

Humph, Kenneth snorted to himself. Of course, belonging to the U.S. would be best. The U.S. could do a lot for Hawaii. The Annexation Club was just trying to help the Hawaiians, that's all. The native Hawaiians just didn't understand. That queen stuff was too old-fashioned.

Then he frowned. But why was Mary so afraid? Were the men in the Annexation Club as bad as Mary said? What were they plotting? And what was this Honolulu Rifles stuff? *You sound like a traitor,* Mary had said.

There was danger here in Honolulu.

3

Guns and Plans

Mary stopped on the sidewalk. Kenneth and Aleesa stopped too. In front of them was a big, white, wooden house. It rose up from a huge, green, rolling lawn. Palm trees framed it.

Aleesa stared. What a house! Her whole family—all her aunts, uncles, cousins—everyone could live in there.

"Is this where we're going?" Kenneth asked. He cleared his throat. The place looked like a hotel.

"This is the Boyds'," Mary said. "Mrs. Boyd is one of the queen's best friends," she added. Then she leaned closer to Kenneth and Aleesa. "But Mrs. Boyd has a big problem these days." Mary made a face. She looked up at the house.

"What's that?" Aleesa asked. This sounded juicy.

"Her nephew lives with her now. Her no-good nephew from the U.S.—Carleton Boyd." Mary scrunched her face up for a second. "He's really scum. Everyone in Honolulu knows it too. His own family sent him here. Away from the U.S. They wanted him out of the way. They hoped he'd stay out of trouble here." Mary shook her head. "But poor Mrs. Boyd."

"So what does he do?" Kenneth asked. What did bad people do in Hawaii in 1893?

"He gets drunk a lot. Causes trouble. Once he even shot at the mules pulling the streetcars in downtown Honolulu. He shot one dead. Poor Mrs. Boyd," Mary said. "The queen worries about her too. That Carleton should go back to the U.S." She frowned.

Carleton sounded like a jerk, Aleesa thought. She hoped she wouldn't run into him. That was for sure.

Kenneth shook his head. This Carleton guy sounded like he was out of control. Kenneth flexed his fingers. He'd take care of Carleton. He didn't do all that weight-training for football for nothing.

Mary, Kenneth, and Aleesa walked up the front walk. Together they mounted the steps. A maid opened the huge front door. She smiled and invited them in.

"I'll take these to Mrs. Boyd," Mary told Kenneth and Aleesa. She took sheets of paper from her basket. "You can wait here in the front hall."

Mary dropped her hat on a chair. Then she disappeared down a long hallway.

Kenneth and Aleesa sat down on a striped sofa. Huge palm trees in pots stood in the hall. Dark brown pictures of stiff-looking men and women lined the walls.

Suddenly, men's voices rose from the next room. The angry sounds filtered through the closed door.

"Listen," Aleesa whispered. She got up. She walked quietly to the door.

Kenneth got up quickly. Aleesa better not get them into trouble, as usual. He'd better be ready to stop her if she did something dumb.

The voices got louder.

"I tell you, these Hawaiians are stupid. They don't deserve to rule themselves," said one voice.

Another voice added, "They're savages. And the queen still has too much power."

"She is causing more problems for us Americans," someone said. "She's backward."

"That's why we began the Annexation Club!" another voice said.

Kenneth and Aleesa stared at each other. "Men from

the Annexation Club are here?" Aleesa asked. "That's that secret club, isn't it?"

"Yeah. And they're *against* the queen," Kenneth said. "They want the kingdom to end. They want to be part of the U.S. Mary said so. But Mrs. Boyd is a *friend* of the queen. What are they doing *here?* Who would let people like that in here?"

Then they looked at each other. "Carleton!" they said at the same time.

Another voice said, "We need to be part of the U.S. We can't trust the queen. Think of King Kalakaua. He signed the treaty with the U.S. Remember?"

Voices agreed loudly.

The man's voice went on. "The U.S. Navy would get to use Pearl Harbor for seven years. And in return, we'd get no taxes on our sugar. But then the U.S. changed its mind. It passed that tax law. The McKinley tariff. And it *still* has the lease on Pearl Harbor. It's Kalakaua's fault. And the queen is worse. She won't help us businessmen. She doesn't care."

"That's right," someone else said. "We sugar planters can't make money. Not since the McKinley tariff. Now no country is taxed—and that hurts *us!*"

"Yes! Hawaii planters are in trouble!" another voice chimed in. "Other countries can grow sugar cheaper. It costs us more. And now we have to sell for less. We're losing money on all the sugar we send to the U.S. We've already lost 12 million dollars. Everyone else is making more money than we are. If we were part of the U.S., we'd get extra money. We'd make money again."

Kenneth whispered, "Somebody sure wants money around here."

"And they don't care about the Hawaiians, either," Aleesa answered.

Just then, a loud voice broke in. "We have to overthrow the queen. We must get rid of her. For good. Those of us here in this room can take care of that. And it's a good thing the Annexation Club is going to have help for the revolt."

Another voice laughed. "The best help we could have too!" More voices laughed.

Aleesa and Kenneth stared at each other. What help could that be? Kenneth asked himself. Who was going to help the Annexation Club revolt against the queen?

The laughter died down. Someone said, "We will win. We will definitely win. And our guns will help. He'll tell us when to use them. He'll send a note. That's our plan."

"Then it's finished for the queen. We can do what they can't do!" another voice said. "We'll need those guns for that."

Aleesa's eyes got wide. "Guns?" she whispered. This was sounding worse. This was dangerous. She didn't want to be here. How were they going to get out of this? How were they ever going to get home?

Guns? Kenneth repeated to himself. Were these men

planning to kill the queen? And here they were, right in the middle of it.

In shock, Kenneth and Aleesa dropped back down on the sofa. The men's voices lowered. But they could still hear the angry tones. In a few minutes, Mary came down the hall. A tall woman came with her. The woman smiled at them.

"Hello, Kenneth and Aleesa," she said. "I'm Mrs. Boyd. Welcome to Honolulu."

"Hello," Kenneth and Aleesa said together. Did Mrs. Boyd know some men from the Annexation Club were right in the next room?

Just then, voices got louder. Mrs. Boyd sighed. "Carleton brings the rowdiest friends over here," she said. "I wish he would settle down." She shook her head.

Kenneth and Aleesa glanced at each other. Poor Mrs. Boyd didn't understand.

"Tell the queen the *lei* will take a few months," Mrs. Boyd said. "But I'll visit her this week as usual. Goodbye." Then she walked down the hall.

"Mrs. Boyd's making a feather *lei* for the queen," Mary said. "She is so nice. But then, the queen is so good to her. The queen is good to everyone," Mary added. "Let's go."

Kenneth and Aleesa stood up. Well, if Kenneth wasn't going to say anything to Mary, *she* was! Aleesa told herself. What they'd heard was terrible! Her heart still pounded.

The maid let them out. They hurried down the steps.

"Mary!" Aleesa burst out. "You should have heard them! Those were some men from the Annexation Club—"

"Shhhhh!" Kenneth and Mary said at the same time. The three stopped on the sidewalk along Beretania Street. A few people crossed the street. But no one came near them.

"Those guys are dangerous," Kenneth said sternly. He frowned at Aleesa. "Watch what you say!" He clenched his fists and looked around them quickly.

"You don't know who can hear," Mary warned. She held the basket tightly.

Kenneth thought for a moment. Those Americans were evil. And he'd been wrong. The Annexation Club wasn't looking out for the native Hawaiians at all. Hah. They cared only about themselves. That was pretty clear. He frowned. Maybe becoming part of the U.S. hadn't been such a great thing at the time. Not if this was the way it had happened.

"Sorry," Aleesa mumbled. She shot a glance full of daggers at Kenneth. He couldn't tell *her* what to do.

"What do you mean—men from the Annexation Club?" Mary asked. She gripped the basket even tighter. "There were some Annexation Club men at the Boyds'?" Her forehead creased in a worried frown.

"They were saying awful stuff," Aleesa said. "They want to get rid of the queen," she breathed. "It sounds like they want to kill her."

"They said the Annexation Club was going to get help from a man somewhere. 'He'—they kept saying. Who's 'he'? And stuff about guns too," Kenneth added. "What can we do?"

"I wonder why they were at the Boyds'?" Mary asked. Kenneth opened his mouth to say "Carleton," but stopped.

"Mary Puanani," a rude voice broke in from behind them. Kenneth looked around. A red-faced young man staggered toward them. His shirt was rumpled. His tie was crooked.

"Hush," Mary said quickly. "That's Carleton Boyd."

Aleesa studied him. Carleton had blond hair and little, beady blue eyes. He even *looked* mean.

So that was Carleton Boyd, Kenneth thought. Humph. Looked kind of wimpy to him. But that was the dangerous kind. Those losers always thought they had to make up for being wimpy. So they acted tough. They did stupid things. Violent things. He shook his head.

"Here," Carleton said. He held out Mary's bonnet. "You forgot this." He tossed his blond hair out of his eyes. He swayed a little. "I wanted to send the maid with this. But Aunt Margaret told me to bring it." He curled his lip.

Then for the first time, he noticed Aleesa and Kenneth. "And who are your—uh—friends?" he asked nastily. He jutted his chin into the air.

She'd like to slap him, Aleesa thought. What a scumbag.

Kenneth clenched his fists. Calm down, he told himself. He'd only make a bad situation worse.

"Kenneth and Aleesa," Mary mumbled. "They're from Maui," she added. She looked down at the pavement.

"Really!" Carleton drawled. "Country bumpkins, eh? Are they helping take care of your wonderful ruler?" he asked sarcastically. "The one who thinks she knows everything? Like how to handle the Royal Kingdom of Hawaii?" he sneered. "The one who's making all the sugar planters go broke? My loving aunt's dear, dear friend—the *queen?*"

Kenneth looked at Mary. She stood silent. Her face was red above her collar. Well, someone had to take control of this. And Aleesa looked as if she was ready to tell Carleton off. That would be disaster.

"Um, we were just on our way," Kenneth said quickly. "Nice to meet you," he lied.

He grabbed both Aleesa and Mary by the arms. He almost pulled them across Beretania Street. He could see the palace tower. They needed to get back there.

"We've got to tell the queen," Aleesa managed to burst out. "You know. What we heard." She looked wildly at Mary. "Doesn't the queen know she's in danger?"

"Yes," Mary said softly. "But I don't think she believes anything will really happen. And she has much courage. She is not afraid.

"Besides, the United States said it would protect the

kingdom. And," Mary added, "the British did too."

"There's something weird going on then," Kenneth said firmly. They walked through the gardens toward the palace. "The Annexation Club guys seem to think they can really get rid of the queen. They're going to have help. Why are they so sure they'll win?" he asked.

Mary looked puzzled. "I don't know," she said.

She pointed to guards standing in front of the palace. They stood at attention, holding rifles. "The palace guards are always ready. And the Honolulu Rifles are *supposed* to be on the queen's side." She frowned. "But they're really not." She sighed.

Kenneth looked at the guards. There couldn't be that many guards, could there? Could they protect the queen? What was the Annexation Club's secret? Why were they so sure they would win? Who was going to help them?

Together, Aleesa, Kenneth, and Mary walked through the huge iron gate. Mary kept talking worriedly.

"I can't believe Carleton Boyd would betray his aunt like that," she said. "I mean . . . she and the queen are close friends. How can he be part of a group to get rid of his aunt's friend?" She shook her head. "He really is awful."

They mounted the stone steps leading to the palace door. Uh-oh—the palace. The royal palace. Aleesa looked at Kenneth. Her heart beat fast.

She looked back at the guards. This was unreal. What were they going to do now? Would they be caught?

Would they throw her and Kenneth in jail?

Kenneth glanced at Aleesa. Then he stared up at the huge palace doors. In just a second, they would be inside Iolani Palace. He looked at the guards. They stood at attention, holding bayonets.

What was going to happen to them?

4

Caught!

"Oh, my gosh," Aleesa whispered. She looked all around. "This is all right!"

Inside the palace, Kenneth's eyes widened. Carved wooden doors and staircases gleamed. Rich-looking vases sat on tables. Gold-framed pictures hung on the walls. Servants in uniforms walked silently through the halls. Well-dressed men and women talked quietly in small groups.

"Holy cow," Kenneth said. "This *is* a palace." The royal palace of Hawaii wasn't any grass hut. That was for sure. This was pretty uptown.

"Come," Mary said. "You need to meet the queen." She led them to a room off the main hall. "And you can tell her what you heard. The Annexation Club, you know?"

"The queen?" Aleesa squawked. "Nuh-uh. I'm not meeting any queen!" She stopped.

"Come on!" Kenneth said through clenched teeth. He pulled at Aleesa. Slowly, she began walking. He walked next to her, holding on to her elbow.

"Wait here a minute," Mary said. She went inside a doorway. Kenneth and Aleesa waited outside.

Kenneth hissed in her ear. "You idiot. That's what we're *supposed* to be doing. Waiting on the queen. Did you forget? You'll get us in trouble yet!"

Aleesa stuck her tongue out at him. "You just think you know everything. You're no Einstein. Didn't you say you thought Hawaii should be part of the U.S.?" Aleesa's eyes narrowed. "That almost got us in trouble with Mary. Not to mention what the queen would say!"

Kenneth turned down the corners of his mouth. "Fine. Fine. I don't think so anymore. Just you be quiet. Hear?"

Be quiet, he'd told Aleesa. But—what was he going to say? What if the queen asked them questions about Maui? Or anything? What could they say? They'd be caught.

He felt a stab of panic. All those guards standing outside. They had bayonets on their rifles too. Would the queen think they were spies plotting to get rid of her?

Mary appeared at the door. "Come in," Mary said. She smiled. "The queen wants to meet her new attendants." She led them inside.

Aleesa gasped. "Oh!" she exclaimed. The walls were covered in blue silk. The curtains were blue. Gold chairs with blue cushions lined the walls. Pictures of royalty hung everywhere.

So many people, Kenneth thought. So where was the queen? What were those red and yellow feathery things on poles those kids were holding? The feathery things looked kind of like flags. They looked important.

That must be the queen, he thought. She sat on a chair. She talked to four men. She held her head high. She listened carefully as one man began talking.

"I don't know if you should, Your Majesty," the man said. "Yes, the native Hawaiians are not happy. The Bayonet Constitution is unfair to them." He put his hands behind his back. He began to pace back and forth. "But don't announce your *new* constitution now. It will cause problems. I think you should wait."

"But my people need it," the queen said. Her eyes flashed. "They must have their rights. They must be able to vote. They have sent me hundreds of petitions."

Another man said, "Listen, please, Your Highness. There have been so many problems lately." He folded his arms. He lifted his chin. "The legislature is not happy with you. The opium bill is a problem. So is the lottery bill. Saying you plan to have a new constitution will only make things worse. They voted down the new constitution idea."

Opium? Lottery? What was going on? Kenneth wondered.

The queen frowned. "I must think of my people," she repeated. "I would do anything for them. They must have a new constitution. The Bayonet Constitution must go. I will announce my new constitution on Saturday."

Kenneth and Aleesa looked at each other. The queen was pretty strong, Kenneth thought. He looked at her with respect.

No wonder Mary liked the queen so much, Aleesa told herself. She was tough.

"Are we supposed to bow, or something?" Aleesa whispered. "Will we mess up?" Her stomach felt as if there were a huge clamp inside. A queen. She was going to have to talk to a queen. But she wouldn't say much. And *she* wasn't going to say anything about the guns and stuff they heard. Let Kenneth do that.

"I don't know," Kenneth said in a low voice. "Just watch, okay? See what Mary does."

Mary walked up to the queen. She bowed her head. Then she motioned to Kenneth and Aleesa. They came closer.

Kenneth poked Aleesa's side. "There. See?" he whispered. "Just bow a little." If only he felt as smart as he sounded.

"Your Royal Highness," Mary was saying. "These are the new members of your household. Kenneth and Aleesa. They are from Maui," she finished, smiling.

Heart thumping, Aleesa bowed. "Ma'am," she mumbled. What was she supposed to say?

She looked at the queen. Kind brown eyes smiled at her.

"Welcome to Iolani Palace. Welcome to my household," the queen said graciously. She waved a hand at the four men. "These men are my cabinet ministers."

"Your Majesty," Kenneth said. He bowed his head. Hah! he thought. That'll show Aleesa. He remembered that from some movie he saw.

"Welcome," the queen repeated. She gestured to some chairs. "You will be shown your duties later. Right now, I want to hear about Maui." She smiled at them.

Kenneth stood rooted to the floor. What now? He didn't know anything about Maui. He couldn't even spell it.

Aleesa's jaw dropped. Maui? This was horrible. What would they say?

"Actually, Your Highness," Mary said, "Aleesa and Kenneth heard something today. They want to tell you about it." She looked at Kenneth and Aleesa.

At least Mary changed the subject. Kenneth cleared his throat. "Uh, we heard some men in the Annexation Club," he said.

The queen's face darkened. "Yes?" she asked. Her mouth tightened.

"They said some things. Some of them were pretty mad. They said they had guns. They want to—uh—get rid of you," Kenneth said.

This was embarrassing. He was having to tell a queen people didn't like her. But there was more.

"Uh . . . they said they were going to have help. The best help there was. But we didn't hear the man's name. And there's a group of people to help too. But we didn't hear who they were either," Kenneth finished.

Whew. That was about it. He felt sweat bead on his forehead. He glanced at Aleesa.

"Yeah, that's what we heard, for sure," she chimed in. She gave him a thumbs-up sign. Kenneth held back a sigh. "For sure?" No one said that in Hawaii in 1893. She'd better watch out.

The queen sat still. Her forehead creased in thought. She looked at the four cabinet ministers standing there.

"Do you know anything about this?" she asked them. "These guns? This help they're getting?"

"No, Your Majesty," one said. "But we all know what the Annexation Club wants to do. Powerful businessmen are in it. People are not happy, you know."

The queen frowned. "Humph," she snorted. "People who are not native Hawaiians. Or Hawaiian citizens, you mean. They are foreign businessmen. And some are grandsons of missionaries too. *They* should know better. There is no love there."

Then the queen looked at Kenneth and Aleesa.

"Thank you for telling me this. I would need more facts before I could do something," she said. Looking at the men, she said, "I want more information. But until I get it, I will not act. I want to keep my people safe. I will not put their lives in danger."

She looked back at Kenneth and Aleesa. "Thank you," she said. She smiled. "Mary will take you to your rooms now," she said. Then she turned to the four men again.

"Okay," Kenneth said. They followed Mary down some long halls. They went downstairs.

"Just a minute," Kenneth said. Mary and Aleesa stopped. "We need to help the queen. Those guys in the Annexation Club are jerks. Let's try to spy on them again. Let's get some more facts for the queen. I want to find out who is helping the club."

Mary almost shook. "No!" she exclaimed. "That's too scary. I can't do that." She twisted her hands together.

"Yeah!" Aleesa said. "Let's do that!" She clasped her hands together. The Hawaiians shouldn't lose their queen! They needed their rights back! Maybe she and Kenneth could even change history. Goose bumps rose on her arms. That would be awesome!

Kenneth grinned at her. "All right." He looked at Mary. "Where would the Annexation Club men hang out?" he asked.

"Hang out?" Mary looked puzzled. "No one is hanging them!" She stared at Kenneth and Aleesa.

Kenneth felt like kicking himself. He had warned *Aleesa* about saying stuff. And *he* almost messed up instead.

"Um . . . I meant, where do some of the members go?" he asked. He cleared his throat. Maybe Mary would forget about what he had said.

"Well," Mary said. "A lot of them are in the legislature. They would be at Government House. On King Street. That's a couple of blocks away." She rubbed her hands together. "But you must be careful," she said. "Those men are powerful. It could be dangerous."

"No problem," Kenneth said. He looked at Aleesa. "Let's go to Government House. Let's hang . . . um . . . stand around. Maybe we'll find something out." They could help the queen! he thought. Maybe—could they— even change history?

"You have some time before the queen needs you," Mary said slowly. "If you're not back in two hours . . ." She stopped. Her face twisted with worry.

"We'll be fine," Kenneth said. He turned to Aleesa. "Let's go!" he said.

Kenneth and Aleesa hurried toward Government House. "Hey, wait," Aleesa said. "Look. There are some pretty flowers." She stopped next to some bushes. She bent down. She picked white flowers. Then she added pink ones. "Pretty, huh?"

"Yeah, yeah, yeah," Kenneth said. "Come on." They walked up the steps of Government House. It was a huge building. It had white columns in front. Guards stood there too. Were they on the queen's side? Aleesa wondered.

Inside the halls, men wearing suits walked and talked together. Some went inside rooms. Others stood in the hall.

"Let's see if we can find some of those jerks," Kenneth said. He pulled Aleesa's arm.

"Okay!" she said. She shook her arm free. "But how?"

"Just listen to what they're saying. Then we can tell if they're club members," Kenneth said. Aleesa just didn't think sometimes. "Did you think they'd be wearing name tags?" he joked.

"Oh, you're funny," Aleesa snapped. But she slowed down next to Kenneth.

A small group of men was heading into a room. Lots of men were sitting in the room already. Was that meathead Carleton Boyd in there? Aleesa wondered.

Kenneth grabbed Aleesa's arm. The small group stopped. Their voices were low. He strained his ears.

"—Club!"

"—and get a note from him."

"—a good plan for annexation."

"There!" Kenneth whispered. He nodded his head toward the men. "Let's listen outside the door."

Together, Kenneth and Aleesa tiptoed toward the open door. Chairs scraped on the floor. Papers shuffled.

The men must be sitting down.

"We must wait for his note to come to Boyd," one voice said. "He said he'll send it to Boyd at home. Then we'll know where to meet them. He won't choose the time or place until the last minute. Then we'll be there with our guns. We can support them. We can overthrow the queen. We can take care of her for good."

Who were they talking about? Kenneth wondered. Who was sending the Annexation Club a note? And who were "them"—the people the men were going to meet?

"Boyd will distribute the guns. He'll have the list," another voice said.

"Who are *you?*" an angry voice demanded behind Kenneth and Aleesa. A hand grabbed Kenneth's shoulder. He froze. Aleesa stiffened.

Aleesa and Kenneth turned around. A red-haired man stood there. "Spying, eh?" he spit out. "Well, we'll see about that." He grabbed their arms. He pushed them into the room.

Thoughts raced through Kenneth's mind. Aleesa stifled a whimper of fear. The men in the room looked up at them. A heavy silence fell over the room.

In fright, Kenneth scanned the faces. Was Carleton Boyd there? He knew they were on the queen's side. If he was there, they were doomed.

Carleton would know they were spying for the queen.

5

The Plot!

No! Kenneth realized. His head felt light. He checked the faces again. No Carleton Boyd. So no one knew who they were. Maybe they could get out of this. But how?

Aleesa stared in fright. Her hands clutched the flowers tightly. No Carleton Boyd? But what could they do now? It still looked as if they were spying.

Suddenly, Kenneth grabbed the flowers from her hands. "Um, we . . . we're bringing these flowers," he stammered. "Delivering." He looked at the man who had brought them in. "Honest!"

The men in the room relaxed. Some of them chuckled. Kenneth and Aleesa glanced at each other.

"We were just trying to find the right room," Aleesa added quickly.

"Fine, fine," the man said. He frowned. "You two should know better than to sneak around. These days, things look suspicious. We can't be too careful." He left them at the door and sat down.

Kenneth and Aleesa fled down the hall. "Good thing I picked those flowers," Aleesa said. She tossed her head and grinned.

"But it was my quick thinking. As usual," Kenneth added. He smirked. Aleesa stuck her tongue out at him.

They hurried back to Iolani Palace. "Let's tell Mary," Kenneth said. "We need to follow Carleton Boyd. We need to know more about this gun plot. We need to find out who it is that's going to send him the note. Maybe—"

Kenneth stopped. He had an idea. He grinned at Aleesa and snapped his fingers.

"Hey, maybe we can stop the note!" he exclaimed. "Then the Annexation Club can't meet the other people. Maybe that will stop them from trying to kill the queen!" His heart raced with excitement.

"Okay," Aleesa agreed. "This really is an adventure!" Her eyes shone. "I want to help the Hawaiians, for sure."

They ran up the palace steps. The royal guards smiled at them. Kenneth and Aleesa entered the palace. They hurried down the gleaming halls.

"No!" Mary said, when they told her their plan. "It's too scary." She put her hand to her mouth. "I . . . I couldn't do that."

"Come on," Aleesa urged. "Don't be such a chicken," she said. She folded her arms and looked at Mary.

"Chicken?" Mary asked, puzzled. "What do you mean—chicken?" She sighed. "They really talk funny on Maui, don't they?"

"Uh, yeah," Kenneth said quickly. "She means why are you so afraid all the time? Don't you want to help the queen?"

"Of . . . of course I do," Mary said softly. "I want to keep Hawaii for us. I don't really want to be afraid." She looked helplessly at Kenneth and Aleesa.

"Well, come on then. You're with us, right?" Kenneth asked. "Nothing will happen to us," he said confidently.

Mary stared down at the floor. Then she nodded slowly. "All right," she said hesitantly. "You're sure things will be safe?"

"No problem," Kenneth said. He sounded braver than he felt.

"Well, Carleton Boyd works on Alakea Street," Mary said. "We can walk there. We can hear what people are saying on the street. And in his office too. Maybe we can follow him and see where he goes."

"Maybe he'll go and talk to the man. The one who's supposed to send him that note," Kenneth said. "The one who sounds like he's in charge of the revolt."

"Oh, sure," Aleesa said. "I'm *sure* Carleton would be that stupid." She looked at Kenneth. She made a face.

"Carleton *is* pretty stupid," Mary said. Then she giggled. The three of them laughed.

Alakea Street was just a few blocks over. It was a busy street. Offices and shops lined the sidewalk. Men walked up and down. Women talked and shopped. Carriages rattled down the street. Mules pulled streetcars on steel tracks.

Weird, Kenneth thought. No cars. And everybody was dressed in those old-time clothes. Kinda funny, though. He had thought here in Hawaii people would be wearing grass skirts. And living in huts. But this looked just like the U.S. Except for the palace.

He looked up and down the street. Hawaii wasn't full of savages. It was civilized. It didn't really need the U.S. to take care of it. It was a good country. And it had a good queen. She'd been nice to him and Aleesa. And she cared about her people. He frowned. They had to try to stop the plot against the queen.

Aleesa looked at a man talking to two uniformed men. The man stood ramrod-stiff in a black suit. He was giving orders of some kind.

"Who's that?" she asked Mary. She pointed across the street.

"That's the U.S. minister, John Stevens," Mary said. "The U.S. sent him here to help Americans. He represents the U.S. president here. The queen told me he used to be a minister to Sweden and Norway. But he got kicked out of those countries. He was a busybody," Mary said. She shook her head. "He sure talks to the queen a lot." She frowned. "Some people are afraid of him."

"Huh," Kenneth said. He looked at Stevens carefully. Then he looked at the men with him. "Those guys. In the uniforms. Are they cops—I mean, policemen?" He winced. Did Mary notice he'd said "cops"?

Mary laughed. "No, those are U.S. Marines. There is a U.S. Navy ship in Honolulu Harbor. It has lots of marines on it. A warship."

"What are they doing here?" Kenneth asked. Marines—and a warship—in the harbor? That didn't sound good for the queen.

"Oh, they're just here to have target practice," Mary said. "They just got back from Hilo. And the U.S. promised to help protect Hawaii. Remember?"

"Against whom?" Aleesa asked. The three walked across the street.

Stevens raised his hand. He adjusted his hat. The marines saluted him. They marched off.

Aleesa watched Stevens walk away. She thought hard. There was something she didn't like about that. Why would the U.S. minister be talking to the marines?

She crinkled her forehead in thought. What did the

textbook chapter say? Wasn't it the marines who landed in Honolulu? Did the marines help overthrow the queen? Why couldn't she remember?

Then her heart skipped a beat. Wait. Stevens was talking to U.S. Marines. If it *was* the marines who took over . . . Oh, my gosh, she thought. Was *Stevens* in on the plot? The U.S. minister himself? She stared while he walked up Alakea Street.

Mary finished fixing her bonnet. Then she went on talking. "The U.S. thinks the British want to take over Hawaii. But then, the British think the U.S. wants to take it over too." Mary grinned. "Everyone wants Hawaii. Pearl Harbor is very important for a navy." Then her face grew serious. "The Annexation Club means business," she said. Her face looked sad again. "We native Hawaiians have lost so much. We don't want to lose our country too."

"I don't want you to either," Aleesa said. Kenneth jabbed her. She scrunched her face up. "I mean . . . I don't want *us* to either."

They stopped in front of a building. Over the door it said "Bardon and Vicar, Accounting."

"This is where Carleton Boyd works," Mary said. She paused. "I . . . I'm not going to go in," she said. "But I'll watch for you."

Kenneth sighed. Just then, Aleesa grabbed his arm.

"Look!" she whispered urgently. She pointed down the street. Kenneth and Mary looked where she was pointing. "Isn't that the guy who caught us spying?" she asked. "The Annexation Club guy?"

"Uh-huh!" Kenneth said. He'd know that bushy red hair anywhere. "And look who's talking to him. Stevens!" he exclaimed. He turned to face Mary and Aleesa. "You know? This is looking kind of suspicious. Don't you think?"

"No joke," Aleesa said. She pressed her lips together tightly. She narrowed her eyes.

"Do you mean you think Stevens is in on the plot?" Mary asked. "The U.S. minister himself?" Her eyes grew wide.

"Makes sense to me," Kenneth said. Then a tiny jolt of fear flickered through him. Could it be? he thought in horror.

"Hey!" Kenneth exclaimed. "I'll bet it's the marines too. Stevens is going to send the U.S. Marines to take over the government. He'll send a note to Carleton so the Annexation Club can join them. With their guns. Then they'll get rid of the queen. It's gonna be like a war!" he said.

"That's right! I remember the chapter now!" Aleesa said excitedly. "That's what the marines did! They landed! They were part of the plot!"

Kenneth caught a glimpse of Mary's face. She looked strange. She was staring at Aleesa.

Aleesa saw Mary staring at her. She froze. Uh-oh! What had she done?

Do something! Kenneth told himself. He couldn't let Mary think about what Aleesa had said. She almost gave them away! Then he began coughing loudly.

"Hack, hack, hack!" His face turned purple. "Aaaaargh! Hack!" He bent over, faking a coughing fit.

"Are you all right?" Mary asked, worried.

Aleesa slapped him on the back. "Come on! Don't choke!" she said. Whew. Kenneth thought pretty fast. Maybe Mary would forget what she had said.

Just then, Kenneth saw something from the corner of his eye. Stevens and the bushy-haired man began walking toward them.

His heart hammered. "Let's get out of here," Kenneth said quickly. "Our new friend is coming. He'll recognize us. I don't want that."

Aleesa, Kenneth, and Mary turned into the nearest shop. It was filled with books and stationery. They stood behind the door. They could see the street through the window. Stevens and the red-haired man stopped in front of the door. Their voices floated in through the open doorway.

"I'll go see the queen," Stevens said. He smiled evilly. "I'll tell her the U.S. will be behind her. I'll say the U.S. will support the kingdom." Then he paused. "She'll never know." He laughed. "And soon, the time will be right for revolt. Just let her try to get rid of the Bayonet Constitution. That will be a good reason to call in the marines. Just wait till the marines land in Honolulu. I'll send Boyd the note. And the Annexation Club will meet us with all their guns."

Aleesa felt an icy chill run down her spine. She shut her eyes.

Fear prickled Kenneth's scalp. This was big-time stuff. Were they in over their heads?

Stevens went on. "It's time the U.S. annexed Hawaii. The Hawaiians can't rule themselves. They're too stupid. Besides, the British might try to take over too. We must move first. And the queen must go. She's standing in the way of good government. But the Annexation Club can take care of that."

Kenneth and Aleesa looked at each other.

"You were right!" Aleesa whispered. "It *is* Stevens!" Her eyes widened in shock.

"The U.S. minister himself! He's going to be part of the revolt!" Kenneth whispered back. His muscles tensed.

"What are we going to do?" Mary asked. She looked from Kenneth to Aleesa.

"I don't know," Kenneth admitted. "But . . . I know one thing." Maybe they couldn't change history, he thought. But they could sure try. "Now we *really* have to do it! We . . . we have to stop Stevens's note from getting to Boyd. We have to stop the Annexation Club. We have to save the queen!"

He slammed his fist into his open hand. He looked at the two girls. "We need to know more though," Kenneth added. "Like when the note will come." And, maybe, they could somehow stop the whole revolt. Could they? Could they change history?

"You're right!" Aleesa said. Kenneth did have good ideas *once* in a while, she snorted to herself. Was there a way to stop the marines from landing too?

"Won't that be dangerous?" Mary asked. Her face looked pale.

Kenneth stared at the two men as they walked away down Alakea Street. He glanced at the shelves of the store. Paper everywhere. That was it—papers! Maybe Carleton had secret papers on the plan hidden somewhere.

"Maybe we can find something out at the Boyds'." He looked at Mary and Aleesa. His voice rose with excitement. "There has to be a plan written down somewhere. Maybe it'll tell us more. We need to sneak into Carleton Boyd's room. We can look for secret papers about the revolt!"

6

Carleton Gets Angry

That night Kenneth, Aleesa, and Mary talked until late. They decided on a plan. But it would have to wait until the next afternoon. In the morning, they had to help the queen.

Morning broke. The Hawaiian sky turned pale blue, then bright blue. Kenneth, Aleesa, and Mary helped bring the queen her breakfast of papaya and breads.

Later, they hurried to the Blue Room. The queen was getting ready to greet visitors for the day. Kenneth and Aleesa followed Mary to the center of the room. Other people came in and out of the room. Maids swept. They dusted. They polished gold and silver. People in fine clothes talked in low voices.

"All right," Mary said to Kenneth. "You hold a *kahili.*" She smiled.

"A *kahili?*" Kenneth repeated. Great. What was that? He looked around the room. How was he supposed to know? What did he do now? Would Mary find out they didn't know anything?

Mary handed Kenneth one of the tall poles with lots of red and yellow feathers on top. "Here," she said. "Stand next to the queen. It's her royal standard."

"Oh, sure," Kenneth said heartily. "Of course. The *kahili.*"

"You hold the other one," Mary said to Aleesa. She handed another *kahili* to Aleesa. "I'll be getting water for the queen. Or anything else she wants."

With any luck, the queen wouldn't talk to them much, Aleesa thought. She walked over to the queen's royal chair. After all, she and Kenneth didn't know anything about anything. She'd hate to get caught now. She wanted to stop the revolt. And now they had a good plan. She really wanted to help the queen and Hawaii.

Kenneth straightened his shoulders. He cleared his throat. Maybe all they had to do was stand here. Maybe they wouldn't have to say anything. That way, the queen wouldn't find out who they were. Or—who they *weren't*. And then they could begin their own plan this afternoon. Could they stop the revolt? Could they change history? Kenneth took a deep breath.

They watched the queen come in. Everyone stood. They bowed. Kenneth and Aleesa bowed too. They looked at each other. Aleesa's eyes were wide. Kenneth cleared his throat.

Would they be able to get through this? Kenneth wondered. Or would the queen discover they were fake?

The queen smiled at Kenneth and Aleesa. "Good morning," she said kindly. "Our new friends from Maui," she added.

You bet, Kenneth thought. He swallowed hard.

"Your new ministers, Your Majesty," a voice announced from the door. "Mr. Peterson, Mr. Colburn, Mr. Parker, and Mr. Cornwell."

Kenneth turned. Four men in suits came in. They weren't the same ministers he'd seen the other day. They walked toward the queen. They bowed.

"Who are these new guys?" Kenneth whispered to Mary. She sighed.

"The poor queen," she whispered. "The Bayonet Constitution took all her power. So the legislature gets to pick her ministers. She can't choose ministers *she* thinks would be the best. The legislature keeps voting them out. Especially if they help the queen."

That was pretty unfair, Aleesa thought. She looked at the four men. The queen couldn't even have advisors she trusted or thought were good for the kingdom.

"Your Highness," Mr. Peterson began. "The legislature passed the opium bill. You need to sign it. The lottery bill passed too. You need to sign that." He glanced at the other three ministers. He handed the queen sheets of paper.

The queen frowned. She drew herself up in her chair. "I do not want to sign the opium bill," she said. "I do not want to have opium licensed for sale." She shook the papers. They rattled in her hand.

One of the other ministers stepped forward. "But, Your Majesty," he began. "The legislature passed it. It is a way to control the smuggling of opium."

Aleesa saw the queen's mouth tighten. This was a big deal, she thought. The queen was pretty much stuck in a trap.

The minister went on. "You know Hawaii's had many problems. And it's because of opium smuggling. This way, maybe we can stop some of it."

Another minister said, "Besides, if you don't sign it, there will be more trouble." He folded his arms across his chest.

The third minister added, "You know, the legislature isn't happy with you right now. They think it was wrong to want a new constitution."

The queen's eyes narrowed. But she said nothing.

"The lottery bill," the last minister said. "The lottery bill will help the monarchy. It will give you more money. The Hawaiian people won't be taxed so much."

Mr. Peterson said, "Your Majesty, you must sign these bills into law."

Kenneth looked at the queen. Things were pretty bad. Ministers could tell the queen what to do. He frowned.

The queen lifted her chin. Her eyes flashed. "I see you leave me no choice." She looked at Mary. "The pen, please."

Mary handed her a pen. The queen signed the two bills. She shook her head.

The queen was proud, Aleesa thought. The queen knew what the Hawaiian people wanted. She wanted to do the right things for them. Aleesa held the *kahili* pole tighter. But the Bayonet Constitution stopped the queen from doing it. She'd sure like to punch those ministers, Aleesa told herself.

The ministers took the papers. Then they talked together in the corner of the room. More people came and talked to the queen.

After a while, the queen smiled at Mary, Kenneth, and Aleesa. "You are dismissed for the day," the queen told them. "Thank you."

Kenneth looked over. The ministers were just getting ready to leave. Yes! he thought. He nudged Aleesa. Then he jerked his head in the ministers' direction.

"Let's follow them," he whispered. His stomach

tightened. Maybe the ministers would lead them to what they needed. The ministers weren't too friendly to the queen.

"Okay," Aleesa agreed. Her heart began to pound. "Come on, Mary," she said in a low voice. "You come too."

Mary looked at the ministers. She shrank back. "I . . . I don't know," she said slowly.

"Come on. We'll protect you," Kenneth assured her. The three followed the ministers out of the Blue Room.

The ministers were strangely quiet. They didn't talk. Their footsteps echoed in the huge hall. They walked out the front doors of the palace. They went down the broad steps. They walked down the long drive.

The bright sunshine almost blinded Kenneth, Aleesa, and Mary. "Hurry!" Kenneth said. "We have to catch up!" They walked so fast they almost ran right into the four men.

The four men had stopped. They stood by the iron gates leading to the palace. Some other men joined them.

Kenneth ducked behind a tree. Mary and Aleesa followed.

"Look!" Kenneth whispered. "It's Stevens! And some other men!" Aleesa's jaw dropped. Sure enough, Kenneth was right. Mr. Stevens, the U.S. minister, was meeting the queen's ministers. The other men clustered around the small group.

"She signed the bills," a voice said. "The lottery and the opium bill both."

"The lottery bill is an attack on the U.S. government!" a voice said angrily. "The opium bill is a disgrace!"

Kenneth and Aleesa looked at each other. That must be Stevens, Aleesa thought.

"The United States will not support the queen," Stevens went on. "If a group decides to set up a new government, I will not promise to back the queen."

"This is not right. We will leave you. Good day, gentlemen," someone said.

Aleesa, Kenneth, and Mary watched the four ministers leave, shaking their heads. The small group around Stevens kept talking.

"The fact that she signed the lottery and opium bills will make the U.S. worry even more!" someone said.

"The U.S. will think she isn't a good queen!" another one said. "Not to mention she wants to throw out the constitution. It will make the U.S. government agree to annexation. Hah!" They all laughed.

"Well," one voice said. "I think we have her now!" The men all laughed again.

"It's up to the U.S. Marines now. And the Annexation Club," said a voice.

It *was* the marines! That's who Carleton's friends would meet! Kenneth and Aleesa stared at each other.

"Just wait until she announces her new constitution on Saturday," said another. "And gets rid of the Bayonet Constitution. It will make all the foreign businessmen angry. And the U.S. will think she's getting out of control."

"Perfect," a voice said. "Just perfect. The Kingdom of Hawaii will soon be no more."

"When Carleton Boyd gets the message you'll send, it'll be done!" someone added.

Aleesa shivered. These men sounded so cold-blooded. She glanced at Mary. Mary's face crumpled. Her eyes filled with tears.

The men said their good-byes and left.

Kenneth frowned. "Let's get to our plan," he said. "Let's get to the Boyds'."

They walked quickly up Richards Street. They crossed Beretania Street. One more block, and the Boyds' house stood in front of them.

"Do you think our plan will work? Will they really believe us?" Mary asked. She twisted her hands as they walked.

"Sure," Kenneth answered. "All we have to do is act like we know what we're doing," he said to Mary. "You told us the queen loves music. She's written good songs. Like 'Aloha Oe,' right? So of course she'd want to borrow a songbook."

The maid answered the door. "Good afternoon," she said, smiling. "Here from the palace?" she asked.

"Uh, yes," Kenneth said quickly. He looked at Mary. She looked at the ground. Kenneth took a deep breath. "The queen sent us," he lied. "She wants to borrow a songbook from Mrs. Boyd."

"Of course," the maid said. "Mrs. Boyd is not at home. But you can go into the study. That's where the songbooks are. Do you know the name of it?"

"No," Aleesa said. "It has some special songs in it. We're supposed to look," she added. She glanced at Mary. Mary's face was bright red.

"Fine," the maid said. The three followed the maid to the study. Kenneth looked around the corner. Yes! Mary was right. Carleton's room was right next to the study!

"Now, you two look through the shelves," Kenneth said. "I'll sneak into Carleton's room. I'll go through everything. Maybe we can find papers about the plot."

"I . . . I hope Carleton doesn't catch you!" Mary said. Her face twisted with worry. "Sometimes he leaves work early."

"Yeah. Probably to go get drunk," Aleesa said. She laughed. Kenneth laughed too. Mary added a feeble giggle.

"Hurry," Kenneth said. "And just pick out any old songbook," he added.

"I'll keep a watch on the door," Aleesa offered. "If anyone comes, I'll say, 'Oh! Look at *this* one!' That'll be your clue to get out of Carleton's room."

"Good idea," Kenneth said. He walked quietly into the room next door. He began pulling drawers open. He shuffled papers. He looked under the bed. He looked behind furniture.

Meanwhile, the girls looked through the books on the shelves. They turned pages. They read titles aloud.

Aleesa kept glancing toward the door. But no one surprised them.

Finally, Kenneth joined them. He sighed. "No luck," he said. "I looked everywhere. There just wasn't anything."

Aleesa had a songbook tucked under her arm. "Well, we got something. Let's go," she said.

They thanked the maid. Walking quickly, they got back to the palace.

"Why couldn't we find anything?" Kenneth asked. He shoved his hands into his pockets. "We just know there has to be something written down."

"Maybe we just didn't look in the right place," Aleesa suggested. If only they had found something. Then it might be easier to stop Stevens's note. Then they could save the queen.

A few hours later, Aleesa, Kenneth, and Mary went to the kitchen for dinner. They sat at the big table with the rest of the queen's attendants.

Suddenly, a housekeeper appeared at the kitchen door. Her eyes were wide with fright.

She stared at Kenneth, Aleesa, and Mary.

"You young people," she said, shaking. "Mr. Carleton Boyd is at the door. He is demanding to see you. He is very angry!"

Kenneth felt the blood drain from his face.

7

The Snoops

The kitchen was deadly silent. Everyone stared at the three of them.

Kenneth stood up. His heart hammered. Kenneth steeled himself. Here it came, he told himself. But he had to be tough.

Her mouth dry, Aleesa got up. She followed Kenneth. Mary was the last one out the door. She almost whimpered.

In the servants' upstairs hall, Carleton Boyd paced up and down. His face was red. His hair was uncombed. His jacket was unbuttoned. He whipped around to face them.

"*You!*" he roared. "I heard you were at the housh today. And shomeone was in my room! I know it!" he yelled. "Everything is a mesh!" He leaned against the wall with one hand.

"Not true!" Kenneth said loudly. He wasn't going to let this loser shout him down. And he didn't leave a mess. He was just like those cop guys on TV. No one could tell he'd been in there. Carleton was just paranoid.

"We were in the study," Aleesa said. She lifted her chin. Her insides were turning to jelly. But she wouldn't let this jerk know it. "We weren't in your room. Besides," she challenged. "Why would we want to go in there, anyway?"

"My papersh. My pershonal papersh!" Carleton shouted. He waved his arms wildly.

Phew! Aleesa thought. Alcohol. She almost had to turn her head. Carleton had really been into the booze before he came. He was out of control.

"What do you mean?" Kenneth asked. "Personal papers?" He tried to look innocent. Hah. Carleton had been hitting the bottle pretty good. He could tell that. Maybe Carleton was dumb enough and drunk enough to say something about the plot.

"In my deshk! I can tell you found the shecret drawer!" Carleton roared. He pounded on the bannister.

Aleesa and Kenneth exchanged glances. Yes! Aleesa thought. Now we know! She hid her grin.

All right! Kenneth told himself. But first they had to get themselves out of this.

He thought fast. "Look!" he said. "Mary wouldn't do that. You don't know us. But you know Mary. How can you think that?"

Next to him, Mary shook like a leaf. But she spoke up. "That's . . . that's right. How . . . how can you say that?" she stammered. "We . . . we were looking for a songbook for the queen. We don't go snooping!" she said. "You . . . you know *me,*" she added.

Carleton snorted. "Huh," he exclaimed. He peered at the three with his reddened eyes. "You're right." He blew his nose on his sleeve. "You wouldn't try anything," he said. "Timid as a moushe," he taunted. "No backbone. No gutsh. Just like all the Hawaiians," he said. He smirked.

Aleesa drew her breath in sharply. She glanced at Mary. That was a nasty comment. She'd like to slap Carleton. Hard. She clenched her fists behind her apron.

Mary swallowed hard. She looked down at the ground.

An angry pulse beat in Kenneth's forehead. He'd sure like to pop him one. But that wasn't the way to win. He looked at Aleesa quickly. Thank goodness. She looked like she was holding in her anger too.

"We're going to get back to our dinner," Kenneth informed him. "Come on," he said, with a bravery he didn't feel. He tugged at Aleesa and Mary. They left Carleton standing in the hall.

"Well, you finally got tough," Kenneth said to Mary. He grinned. He wiped his forehead. That had been a close one.

"Tough?" Mary asked. "What do you mean?" They walked toward the kitchen.

Uh-oh. Another wrong word. When was he going to remember that it was 1893? People didn't talk like that! He saw Aleesa make a face at him.

"I mean . . . strong. Brave. You know," Kenneth said. They stopped outside the kitchen door.

"Well, you started me thinking. With what you said. You two are really helping. I need to do more too," Mary said. "And I really don't want the queen hurt. Or to lose our country, Hawaii, to the U.S." She sighed. "So I just had to say something."

"All right." Kenneth smiled. "Now, tomorrow we go back to the Boyds'."

"No!" Mary exclaimed. "Carleton will kill us!" she cried. "If he catches us—"

"Nah," Kenneth said. He sounded more confident than he felt. "I know Boyd's type. All talk. We'll look for the papers. Same drill. All right? But this time, I go right to the desk."

"You mean, the *deshk*," Aleesa said. She giggled. Mary did too.

The next afternoon, they stood in front of the Boyds' door. Aleesa swallowed hard. She couldn't believe they were doing this again. She looked over at Kenneth. He gave her a thumbs-up sign. The maid opened the door.

"We're here for another songbook," Mary said. She held out the other songbook to the maid. Her hands trembled a bit. "The queen said this wasn't the right one," she added.

"Of course," the maid said. She led them back to the study. Aleesa and Mary began going through the books on the shelves.

"Go for it," Aleesa whispered. Her heart hammered. They must be crazy to do this.

Kenneth's muscles tensed. He walked quickly into Carleton's room. He felt along each drawer. There! A tiny catch slid open. A secret drawer spilled its contents. His breath came in ragged bursts. This was it!

He scanned the papers. "Opium Customers," read one. Opium! Carleton was selling opium himself? What slime! Another paper was a letter. It was signed "J. L. Stevens, U.S. Minister."

Kenneth dropped down in the chair to read it.

> *We must Americanize the islands. We*
> *must gain control of the crown lands,*

part of it read. Holy cow! he thought. Stevens was definitely plotting against the queen. That was illegal!

He read on.

> *Hawaii must take the road that leads to*
> *America.*

He shook his head.

He shuffled more of the papers from the drawer. Plot. Plot. Plot. Why couldn't he find anything? His heart beat under his shirt. Was there a timetable? When were things going to happen?

There! No date. No time. But a list.

> *Guns handed out to Club. Marines land.*
> *March to Iolani Palace. Annexation Club*
> *meets. End of Queen.*

The words jumped out at him.

> *End of Queen!*

"Look at *this* one!" Aleesa's worried voice called out. Kenneth froze. Oh, no! Their secret phrase! Then he began stuffing papers back into the drawer. There were so many! Help! he cried out silently.

"I *knew* you little rats were up to no good!" Carleton's voice roared at him.

Too late. Carleton stood in the doorway, swaying with drink. Behind him, Aleesa shrank against the wall. Her face was pale. Mary trembled next to her.

"You'll all end up in Honolulu Harbor for this," Carleton threatened. He moved toward Kenneth.

Come on, dodge the blockers, Kenneth told himself. Just like football. He dashed past Carleton to the door. Then he stopped. Wait. He did have something he could use against Carleton. The list.

"You can't do anything," Kenneth blustered. He couldn't let anyone know how scared he was. "We know about the list. The opium list. You try anything and we'll let the queen know," he said.

"If you stay alive," Carleton yelled. He stumbled toward the three of them. He tripped on a chair leg. Thud! He fell to the floor. His eyes closed.

"Unnnnnnh!" he groaned. Then he twitched.

"Let's get outta here!" Aleesa yelled. The three of them raced down the hall. They flung the door open. They rushed down the steps. Charging across Beretania Street, they dodged a streetcar. It just missed them. The driver shook his fist.

Panting, they reached the palace. They skittered down the stairs to their rooms. In relief, they collapsed on some chairs.

Aleesa wiped her forehead. "Great," she moaned. "Now Carleton Boyd is after us," she said. "He'll kill us!" What in the world did she think she was doing? She belonged back home, in Berkeley, California! This was crazy!

Mary's eyes were huge. "Oh, no! No, no, no!" she whimpered. "I don't want to die!"

"Quiet!" Kenneth said. He took a deep breath. "He's got other things to do. Besides, we can't stop now. Tomorrow is Saturday. The legislature ends. Remember? Things will start happening. The queen still wants to announce her new constitution. She'll get rid of the

Bayonet Constitution. That's what she told her other ministers. And I'll bet you anything Stevens will decide the time has come to overthrow the queen. It could be any day now."

Kenneth looked hard at Aleesa and Mary. He doubled up his fists.

"Stevens will probably think *this* is the right time to take over Hawaii. That's what we heard him say in the street. So Carleton will have too much to do. He has guns to hand out. He's got to organize his men. He won't have time for us." He paced up and down. Then he stopped.

"I hope," he added. His heart pounded.

What if Carleton *did* come after them?

8

The Queen Is Betrayed

The queen smiled gently at Kenneth, Aleesa, and Mary on Saturday morning. The hall was crowded outside the Throne Room. She had just come back to the palace. She had been at Government House all morning. The legislature had ended.

"Thank you, my young people," the queen said. "Thank you for trying to help."

Aleesa could hardly hear the queen. Loud music filled the air. The Royal Hawaiian Band was playing. Dozens of people crowded into the red Throne Room. Important people from other countries were there. Legislators were there. The Hawaii Supreme Court was there.

Outside the palace, hundreds of Hawaiians stood. They were all waiting. The queen had said she would make an announcement. Everyone knew it was about her new constitution. No more Bayonet Constitution!

"I know you tried to help," the queen said. She frowned. "If what you just told me is true, many people are traitors."

"Your Majesty," Aleesa began. Maybe the queen would wait. Maybe she'd put off telling people about the new constitution. Then she could get her royal guards ready for the marines. And Aleesa and Kenneth and Mary could still try to stop the note from getting to Carleton Boyd. Aleesa shivered, thinking about Carleton's threat. The marines were bad enough. But what was the Annexation Club planning to do to the queen?

"Maybe—" Aleesa started to say.

"My child," the queen broke in. She smiled. "Do not worry. I have the Hawaiian people behind me. I still cannot believe the United States would make an act of war. I don't believe the U.S. Marines will land." She looked around her. "But I will keep my people safe," she said. "I would give my last drop of heart's blood to keep them safe."

She turned. "I am meeting my ministers now. Before I announce the new constitution. They are waiting in the Blue Room. Come," she said. Kenneth, Aleesa, and Mary followed the queen.

Peterson, Cornwell, Colburn, and Parker waited in the Blue Room.

"Your Highness," Peterson said. He looked uncomfortable, Kenneth thought. Like he had an itch or something. Peterson looked almost guilty. Something wasn't right.

"We, your cabinet ministers, have something to say. We do not think you should announce your new constitution," Peterson said. He cleared his throat. The other three ministers looked at the carpet. "There might be an uprising. The businessmen and foreigners may revolt."

Kenneth saw the queen's face darken. "You have led me out on the edge of a cliff," she said to her ministers. "You told me this would be all right two months ago. Before you were even in the cabinet. I would never have told anyone to be here today. Everyone is waiting to hear the new constitution. Now you are deserting me. I am taking this step alone. It is humiliating."

The queen was proud, Kenneth could see that. The ministers had tricked her. That was unfair. It was wrong.

"Your Majesty," Peterson said. "You must tell the people to wait. It is not wise to announce it today."

The queen tightened her mouth. She frowned. "I will do as you say," she said sternly. She narrowed her eyes. "I will tell everyone to go home. I will tell them to keep the peace. I will tell them I had to give in to my ministers. For now," she added. She lifted her head. She swept from the room. Aleesa, Kenneth, and Mary hurried out the door.

Aleesa swallowed hard. She looked at Kenneth. The queen had guts, she thought.

"Look!" Aleesa said. She elbowed Kenneth. "There's Stevens," she hissed. The U.S. minister stood in the hall, talking to a small group of men. The group broke up. Stevens started down the hall.

"Let's follow that jerk," Kenneth whispered. He nodded his head at Stevens. Stevens tipped his hat to some other men. "I have a funny feeling," Kenneth added.

"But what about Carleton Boyd?" Mary asked. "Once we leave the palace, we're not safe!"

"I'm sure Carleton is plenty busy counting out guns," Kenneth answered. "If he's not already drunk somewhere. And as long as we stay in a crowded place, we'll be safe." He frowned. "We've got to know what Stevens is planning. Maybe we can hear more about the revolt. We have to try to stop his note to Carleton. Who knows what Carleton would do—kill the queen?" Kenneth tightened his mouth.

Aleesa crinkled her forehead. "Yeah," she said. "I still can't believe that the queen's ministers backed down like that. The queen said they told her it was okay. Two months ago. But now they've changed their minds. They say it's because they're afraid for her."

"She's almost all alone in wanting the people's rights back," Mary said. "All except for the Hawaiian people."

"Let's go," Kenneth said. They walked silently. They shadowed Stevens out of the palace. He walked to Government House. The three stayed behind him. They kept out of sight.

Aleesa's heart pounded. "Where's he going?" she asked. She kept looking over her shoulder. Carleton Boyd was the last person she wanted to see. They hurried up the steps. She saw Stevens disappear into a room. The door closed.

"Dang!" Kenneth exclaimed. "'We have to hear what's going on." Then he grinned. "I know! Let's go around the outside. The windows are open! Maybe we can hear."

They sneaked around the side of Government House. Kenneth pointed up. "There!" he said. "That should be the window."

Aleesa frowned. "It's up pretty high," she observed. "Wait! I bet I can climb that tree! Even in a long dress!" She looked around quickly. No one was watching. Good! Before Kenneth and Mary could say anything, she scrambled up the trunk.

"Ouch!" she whispered. She'd scraped her shins. She hid in the leaves. No one could see her from the ground. Below her, she could see Kenneth frowning. Mary shrank against the building. She looked worried.

Aleesa strained her ears. Yes! It was a meeting. What were they doing? Bits of conversation floated out the window. She could see just some of the men in the room.

"It's time to plan a new government. One run by *us,* not by a queen."

"Yes. The queen is making a revolutionary act. She wants to get rid of the Bayonet Constitution. That's the best reason for getting rid of *her.*"

Aleesa winced. What did they mean, "get rid of"? Did they plan to kill her? Carleton Boyd would certainly do anything. Especially if he were drunk.

A new voice spoke up. "As the queen's ministers, we must ask you not to do this."

Aleesa held on to the branch tightly. The ministers were there too? They were trying to stop the revolt! Now she saw two of them hunched over the table.

"She has decided to put off a new constitution. You cannot overthrow her," another minister said.

"She has the *attitude* of treason, though," an angry voice said. "She *wants* to get rid of the old constitution."

"Yes, I told you before," Stevens's voice said. "I will recognize the new government. The queen will be committing treason if she announces a new constitution."

"We must go," one of the ministers said. Aleesa heard chairs scrape. A door slammed. The ministers must have given up, Aleesa thought. They were gone.

"They are lost," someone said. "Back to business.

We'll form a Committee of Safety this afternoon. We'll plan a new government."

"We'll ask Sanford Dole to be the new president," someone said. "He might want Ka'iulani, the queen's niece, to be queen. But we'll tell him no more queens or kings. We're going to be part of the United States!"

"I promise you I will make sure the U.S. accepts your new government," Stevens's voice said. "As the U.S. minister, I can do that. And I have the marines."

Oh, my gosh! Aleesa almost fell out of the tree. Stevens was really in charge. He had the threat of the U.S. Marines. He had the U.S. government behind him. Stevens had a lot of power.

"Good," said a man's voice.

"And the marines will back you up. Just be sure you are in control of the government buildings. Then I can say you are the new government. The queen will be out," Stevens said.

"We'll get men together," someone said. "Carleton Boyd will wait for your message."

"I'll send it when I'm ready for the marines to land," Stevens said. He laughed. "Gentlemen—this has been my dream for so long."

Aleesa heard chairs scraping again. Men were getting up.

"I will leave you to your planning," Stevens said. "I will be in touch. Remember, it doesn't matter if the queen changes her mind about the constitution. She is out. This is a great opportunity for us and for you."

Aleesa slithered down the trunk. Her heart raced. She yanked at Kenneth and Mary.

"Come on," she said. "We've got to get back to the palace. The queen must know. This new group—the Committee of Safety. They're planning a new government. They're plotting with Stevens. They're even picking a new president!"

"No wonder everyone's backed out on her," Kenneth said angrily. "The rats. They must know the U.S. government is against her. Not to mention the marines too."

"The poor queen!" Mary wailed. "What can we do?"

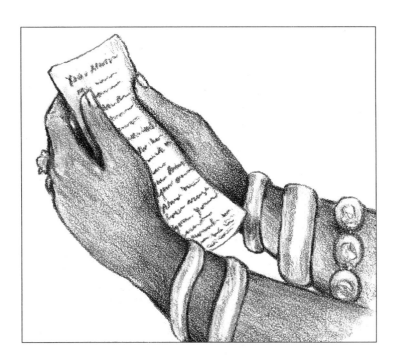

9

The Note

"I'm sorry," the lady-in-waiting told Kenneth, Mary, and Aleesa. She stood at the bottom of the stairs. They were out of breath from their race to the palace. "The queen does not want to be disturbed," the lady said.

"But . . . but we know stuff! We have to tell her! It's danger!" Aleesa burst out.

The lady looked behind her. Then she lowered her

voice. "It is not wise to speak loudly," she warned. "There are enemies even in the palace." Sadness clouded her eyes. "Our brave queen is in danger everywhere," she said.

"But . . . what can we do?" Aleesa begged. "You have to let us talk to her!"

Aleesa, Kenneth, and Mary crowded closer. The lady stepped back. She smiled. "You really want to help, don't you?" she asked. The three nodded. "Well, then. Write her a note. I'll see that she gets it."

"Thank you!" Kenneth said. "We'll bring it to you right away."

After they finished writing it, Mary read the note aloud.

> *Your Majesty: We hate to tell you this. We overheard the U.S. Minister Stevens talking. He was with a group of men. They said they would form the Committee of Safety. It's part of the Annexation Club. But it's more dangerous. The Committee will plan a new government. They've already picked a president. They said they didn't care what you did.*
>
> *Stevens promised them he'd send the U.S. Marines to overthrow the queen. And we think Carleton Boyd is planning to murder you. Please, Your Highness. Maybe you should think about leaving.*

You could hide somewhere.
Respectfully,
Your friends, Kenneth Smith, Aleesa
Strong, and Mary Puanani Hayes

Mary sighed. Her eyes welled with tears. She folded the note up. "I hope she reads it," Mary said. "I hope she pays attention."

"I hope so too," Kenneth said. He leaned back in his chair.

"You know what?" Aleesa asked. "I don't think the queen will listen. I think she's too proud to run. I think she'll stay. She'll support her people to the end."

"Well, if she doesn't get the note, we'll never find out," Kenneth said. They took the note upstairs to the lady.

"I'll see that she reads it," the lady said. "That's all I can do."

All night long, Aleesa tossed and turned. Her sheet was rumpled. She punched her pillow into a little ball. She couldn't sleep. What if the marines landed? Would she, Kenneth, and Mary be in danger too? Would they be thrown in prison?

A sudden thought hit her. She lay still for a moment. What if they *never* got back home? Sure, she wanted to help the queen. But . . . she wanted to go home too. Would she spend the rest of her life in a Hawaiian prison?

In the next room, Kenneth lay awake. The moonlight traced a pattern on the ceiling. How could they stop

Stevens's note from getting to Carleton Boyd? He shut his eyes for a second. It didn't sound like there was any way to stop the marines from landing. But if they at least could stop Carleton, maybe the queen would be safe.

Too soon, the sky lightened. The palm trees no longer looked black against the sky. They became green in the morning light. Kenneth sighed and got up. What did the queen think of their note?

The queen met them after breakfast. She called them into the Blue Room. They bowed. They stood, waiting.

"You three are precious to me," she began. "You love our *aina,* our land, Hawaii. And I appreciate your concern for me."

Uh-oh, Kenneth thought. He looked quickly at Aleesa. She turned the corners of her mouth down. She must be thinking the same thing. The queen wasn't buying it.

"But I will never leave," the queen stated. "I will never leave my people. I would shed my heart's blood for them." She looked gravely at the three of them. "I still cannot believe the United States would betray me. I cannot believe the marines would march on Honolulu."

"But . . . Your Majesty—" Aleesa blurted out. Kenneth jabbed her. He made a quick face at her. Holy cow! She shouldn't interrupt the queen!

The queen smiled. "I know there is plotting. But there has been plotting before too. It will pass," she said. She looked down at the papers in her hand. "I have work to do. I must write the announcement about no new constitution.

My ministers advised me to. They will read it tomorrow, Monday." She nodded her head. "You are dismissed."

Kenneth, Aleesa, and Mary walked slowly from the Blue Room.

"Now what?" Aleesa demanded. She frowned. "How can we save the queen? Or us? What if we get caught in this revolution too? And then we'll never—" She stopped and bit her tongue. And then we'll never get home! she almost blurted out. But she caught herself in time. Whew! She glanced at Mary. Mary didn't notice anything wrong. But Kenneth was shaking his head. They heard footsteps down the hall.

"Look!" Kenneth exclaimed. "'There's Stevens!" They turned to watch Stevens come closer.

"Is he coming to talk to the queen?" Mary asked. "What in the world would he say?"

"Let's find out," Aleesa suggested. They edged closer to the door of the Blue Room.

"Try and look innocent," Kenneth commanded. They changed their faces to smiles.

Stevens began talking. "I assure you, Your Highness, that the United States will stay neutral. I have heard about the plotting. But the U.S. will stay out of it," he said. "I give you my word."

"That snake!" Aleesa hissed. "What a liar! Now the queen definitely won't take any action. She won't get the royal guards ready. Or anything. She trusts people—even Stevens."

"What a jerk," Kenneth agreed. He pressed his mouth into a thin line.

"When do you think he'll send Carleton the note?" Aleesa asked. She slumped against the doorway. Things were looking desperate. And it looked as if they'd never get home. She didn't want to die here in Hawaii.

Killed in a palace revolution in Hawaii, she sighed to herself. No more junk food. No more rap concerts. No more writing notes to Tyleene. No more cute guys at the mall. Sure, she wouldn't have to do her social studies project on native rights either. But she'd definitely rather write a report than die!

"I don't know when he'll send the note. Not yet, I bet," Kenneth said. His mind raced ahead. How would this work? he wondered. "Okay. First, the queen has to tell everyone she'll put off a new constitution. That'll be tomorrow, Monday. We know the Committee of Safety has to take over Government House. That's what Stevens told them to do. Then Stevens will send the marines. That means when the committee moves, we'd better get over to the Boyds'. As fast as we can. Maybe we can stop Stevens's messenger."

"Yeah," Aleesa said. "And hope Carleton doesn't get us first," she added. A twinge of danger rippled through her. She swallowed hard.

They would have to go back to the Boyds' for their plan to work. And Carleton would be there.

10
End of a Kingdom

The rest of Sunday went by slowly. Looking out the palace windows, Kenneth and Aleesa saw men hurrying back and forth on King Street. Royal guards marched up and down Punchbowl Street. The air seemed tense.

Kenneth ran a finger around the inside of his collar. "I don't like this feeling," he whispered to Aleesa.

"I know," she whispered back. "It's as if everyone's

waiting for something to happen." She looked worriedly at Kenneth.

"Yeah," he said. "And we know that it will." He shook his head. "A revolution. And here we are. Right in the middle of it."

"I hope we can stop Carleton," Aleesa sighed. She shivered. "Maybe we can't stop the marines. But we can try to rescue the queen from Carleton and his murdering friends."

"Uh-huh," Kenneth agreed. "We'll have to pay attention. We'll have to beat Stevens's messenger to the Boyds'. So let's hope we can tell when Stevens might call out the marines."

They watched the queen come back from Kawaihao Church. Later, they served tea and biscuits at her meeting. She met with her charity, the Lili'uokalani Educational Society. Mary told them the queen began it. The society gave money to schools for Hawaiian children.

"The queen sure is busy doing good things for other people," Kenneth said, afterwards. "Too bad she doesn't think more about herself," Aleesa said. She frowned.

They watched the queen's ministers as they came in and out, several times. Soon, Sunday was over.

Kenneth, Mary, and Aleesa finished their Monday morning chores in the back pantry. They went to the main hall in the palace.

"What's all that noise?" Aleesa asked. Together, the three looked out a window. Hundreds of native

Hawaiians and others crowded into Palace Square. People were giving speeches.

"We love our queen," a man was saying. Cheers erupted from the crowd. Loud clapping followed.

Mary leaned her head against the window frame. "This is so sad," she whispered. "I just know this is the beginning of the end."

Aleesa patted Mary on the shoulder. "It doesn't look good," Aleesa agreed. And how, she told herself. When were the marines coming? she wondered. Would they know in time to get to the Boyds'?

"Even now," the man went on. "Even now, there is a meeting at the Honolulu Rifles' Armory. They are talking revolution. Against our queen."

The crowd growled and grumbled. Kenneth saw angry faces. Some shook fists.

"The foreigners want to take away our *aina,* our land," the man said. "But we will support our queen."

The crowd roared its approval.

"Long live the queen!"

"The queen! The queen!"

"Hawaii Pono'i!"

Kenneth turned away from the window. "Hey!" he said. "I don't like this. There is a meeting at the armory— against the queen?" he asked. "Aren't there guns at the armory? This looks like it might be the time! We can't take a chance now. They're probably getting ready to march to Government House!"

"You're right!" Aleesa exclaimed. "We'd . . ." she paused. Her mouth felt dry. "We'd better get over to the Boyds'. If Stevens is going to have the marines land, this afternoon looks like a sure bet. It looks like this is coming down now."

"Coming down?" Mary asked. She frowned. "All this Maui talk is funny-sounding."

Kenneth gave Aleesa a little kick when Mary wasn't looking. Aleesa scrunched up her face at him.

"We . . . we really are going to the Boyds'?" Mary twisted her hands together. Her face was pale.

"Look," Aleesa said. She was really getting tired of Mary's whining. "Do you want to try and save the queen?" Aleesa challenged her. "Or not? The U.S. Marines may not hurt her. But who knows what Carleton Boyd will do. Right?"

"Aleesa's right, Mary," Kenneth said. "Once he gets the note, he'll get the Annexation Club to meet the marines. They'll have guns," Kenneth reminded her. "And Carleton is half-crazy. Especially when he's drunk." He folded his arms and looked at Mary.

"Which he probably will be today," Aleesa added. "Wimps like that always have to drink to get their courage up." She frowned. That was a little close to home. That was one reason she lived with Grandma. Her dad used to do that.

"The queen doesn't believe anything will really happen," Kenneth said. "So we're the only ones who can

90

help her." He looked carefully at Mary. Mary bit her lip. Her eyes were on the ground. "Don't you care for the queen?" he asked. "Don't you want to do something for Hawaii?"

"Y-yes," Mary said. She lifted her head. "All right. I'll come too." She sighed.

"Let's get out of here then," Kenneth said. "We better hurry. We might already be too late."

They raced down the back stairs. No one saw them go. Aleesa picked up her long skirts and ran. Long skirts were really a pain, she thought. She was glad she had shorts at home. Home, she remembered. Would they get home? Or would they be shot in the revolution? She shuddered.

They halted at the corner of Beretania Street. "We can't let Carleton see us, dummy," Kenneth said. He grabbed Aleesa's arm. "We'll have to sneak up. Let's hide in the yard next door."

They crossed Beretania. Then they hurried up the block. The Boyds' house loomed ahead. Aleesa's heart raced. Was Carleton looking out the window? Would he make good on his promise about dumping their bodies into Honolulu Harbor?

Sneaking into the yard next door, they found some bushes to hide in.

"Now what?" Mary asked. She scrunched down lower.

"Now we wait for a messenger," Kenneth said.

"Since it's from Stevens, he'll probably have a U.S. flag on the carriage."

He peered down the street. No sign of one yet. Wait! Here came a carriage.

"Now!" he almost yelped. He jumped out of the bushes. He flagged down the carriage. His stomach clamped in fear. Would this work?

"Yes?" a frowning man leaned out the window. "What do you want?"

"The message for Mr. Boyd. From Mr. Stevens," Kenneth said. "Mr. Boyd asked me to get it."

The man stopped for a moment. He looked at Kenneth carefully. "Well," he said slowly. "You *are* just a child."

A child! Kenneth wanted to snap. But he kept quiet. "Yes, sir," he managed to say. Hold on, he told himself.

"You couldn't be in a conspiracy," the man decided. He handed Kenneth an envelope. Kenneth took it, his hands shaking.

"Here," the man said. He smirked. "And my compliments to Mr. Boyd. If he's sober. Let's go, driver," he called out.

The carriage driver cracked the whip. The horses snorted. The carriage rolled off.

"Yes!" Kenneth almost shouted. Mary and Aleesa rushed to join him. "Let's get out of here!" The three raced back to the palace. Aleesa kept looking over her shoulder. Was Carleton Boyd following them? But no one was in sight.

When they got back to the palace, Kenneth opened the envelope. He unfolded the note.

"Listen to this." He began reading.

> *Boyd: The marines will land around 5 p.m. They will march to Government House. Be there with your friends and your guns. Signed, Stevens.*

Kenneth grinned at the two girls. "And it's 4:30 right now. He'll never make it!"

"We did it!" Aleesa crowed. "We rescued the queen!" She wanted to jump up and down. Then she stopped. Voices began shouting in the palace. Footsteps hurried up and down the stairs.

"What's going on?" she asked. She looked down the hall.

"The marines are marching!" a voice yelled. "U.S. Marines are marching in front of the palace!"

Aleesa and Kenneth looked at each other. Aleesa's jaw dropped. Her palms felt sweaty.

"Did we escape Carleton—just to be killed by the marines?" Aleesa asked.

"What do you mean—you escaped Carleton?" an ugly voice said behind them.

Aleesa, Kenneth, and Mary whipped around. No! Kenneth thought. There was Carleton. He must have seen them after all. He had followed them. Now what? Fear stabbed him like a knife. Wait. Carleton couldn't kill them in the palace, could he?

Kenneth straightened his shoulders. He lifted his chin. He had to take care of this jerk.

"Look," he said loudly. "You are a traitor. You should get out of Hawaii. You're a disgrace to the human race," he said.

"Get out of Hawaii!" Carleton began laughing. "Not now. Not when my side is winning!"

"You care nothing for Hawaii and its people," Mary broke in. Her eyes flashed. "You must leave the islands. Or . . . or . . ." she paused. She looked at Aleesa. Help me! her eyes seemed to say.

"Or we'll tell your aunt about the opium list!" Aleesa said triumphantly. "See how much your family likes your little business on the side, you snake!" she said. She put her hands on her hips. She tossed her head. She looked over at Kenneth.

He was grinning at her. Aleesa did pop off sometimes, he thought. But this time it was okay!

Carleton's face turned white. "You won't. I'll . . . I'll . . ." he blustered.

"You'll what?" a woman's voice said behind them. Then Mrs. Boyd swept into the middle of their group.

Finally! Kenneth thought. They'd be safe.

"Uh . . . Aunt! Hello, Aunt," Carleton stammered. "These children were just—"

"They were just telling the truth. I know all about it," Mrs. Boyd said. "Guards!" she called. "I knew somehow it would come to this." Four royal guards hurried up.

94

They clapped handcuffs on Carleton. "You'll be on the next boat out of Honolulu. Your parents can deal with you."

"Yes!" Aleesa burst out. Whew! They were safe! Mary's eyes danced with joy. Kenneth gave her a thumbs-up sign.

"Thank you," Mrs. Boyd said to the three. "Thank you for your help. I thought Carleton got too upset over nothing. He was upset that you three had gone through his things. So I knew something was wrong."

Mrs. Boyd glared at her nephew. "I found the list. And cabled your parents. They know too. They're waiting for you in Ohio. It's going to be a long time before you're free."

The guards led Carleton away. "Unhand me!" he was yelling. "You dogs!"

Mrs. Boyd stared out the window. Her eyes misted with tears. "I can't believe it," she said. "U.S. Marines. And their guns are pointed at the palace gates. They say it's to protect the Americans who live in Hawaii. Because of the queen making a new constitution." She laughed bitterly. "But if that's the reason, why are they *here* at the palace? Why aren't they in front of Americans' homes? To protect them? That's not why the U.S. Marines are here. And we know it."

She shook her head. She wiped her eyes. Then she walked down the hall to see the queen.

Kenneth and Aleesa looked at each other. The

95

textbook had been right, of course. This was the first step. The revolution had started.

The marines set up camp when darkness came. Aleesa and Kenneth watched them. No shots had been fired. Yet.

They spent another sleepless night. Aleesa stared at the ceiling fan above her bed. The blades turned. Whop-whop-whop-whop. What would happen tomorrow?

Why couldn't she remember what happened in the revolution? Had people gotten killed? Were they going to die? And would they ever get back home?

Could she and Kenneth sneak out into the garden and try to find that flower? If they smelled it, could they get home again? They'd done their job, hadn't they? Now would be the time—they'd helped the queen. And gotten rid of Carleton.

In his room, Kenneth stared out the window. In the darkness, he could see the flames from the campfires of the marines. Some were in front of the palace. Some were camped at Government House. He'd heard there were more than 150 armed marines. He swallowed hard. Why couldn't he remember what happened?

Dawn came. The air in the palace was tense. Voices were hushed. Men came and went. The queen was in the Blue Room all day. Kenneth, Aleesa, and Mary took turns looking out the window. The marines marched up and down.

Should they try to leave? Kenneth wondered. But there were marines everywhere. It was too late. If they were going to get shot by the marines, there was nothing they could do.

"This waiting is really bad," Kenneth finally said. He sighed. They sat at the kitchen table. They were polishing silver. But they kept listening to see what would happen next. Would the queen fight back? Would she call the royal guards to fight the marines? He frowned. But there weren't very many royal guards. He tapped a fork on the table. Tap-tap-tap. When would this be over? "I can't stand this waiting," he repeated.

"No kidding," Aleesa grumbled. "But waiting beats getting shot, if that's what's going to happen to us."

"Oh, no! Don't say that!" Mary squeaked. A spoon trembled in her hand.

Finally, at six o'clock, the queen called her staff together in the red Throne Room. Many government people were there. Foreign diplomats were there too. The ministers stood nearby. The queen stood tall. In a clear voice, she began talking.

"I have been told a new government has begun. I have been asked to leave the throne." She lifted her chin higher. "I, Queen Lili'uokalani, yield to the superior force of the United States of America. The U.S. minister, John L. Stevens, caused United States troops to be landed. He said he would support the new government."

She looked at the faces in the crowd. Aleesa followed

her gaze. Only a few people looked happy. Most looked sad. Women were crying. Men's faces were red.

"I yield to avoid bloodshed," the queen went on. "I yield to avoid the loss of life for my people."

"This is the end of the kingdom!" Aleesa whispered to Kenneth and Mary. Mary's eyes filled with tears. To Aleesa's surprise, hers did too.

Stop it, Aleesa told herself. Don't you be crying over this. But she swallowed a lump in her throat. Even in defeat, the queen was royal. She was brave. She still cared for her people.

"It might be the end. But you know?" Aleesa whispered. "We saved her from Carleton and his guns."

"You're right," Kenneth agreed. "We helped to rescue her. At least she's alive."

Kenneth swallowed hard. This was sad, all right. But the queen still had her dignity. Good thing they had stopped Carleton when they did.

———

The next morning, they stood and watched the queen drive away in her carriage. She was moving to her own home. She was leaving the palace.

Kenneth, Aleesa, and Mary waved. They stood with the rest of the staff in the gardens.

"Well," Mary said, sighing. She wiped tears from her eyes. "Guess I'll go pack. Time to go home to Kauai." She looked at Kenneth and Aleesa. "You're going back to Maui, right?"

"Uh-huh," Kenneth said quickly. He shot a glance at Aleesa. Don't say anything, he warned silently.

"I just want to take one more walk in the gardens," Aleesa said. She poked Kenneth.

"Okay," he said. "Bye, Mary." He raised a hand.

"Bye," Aleesa said. "Maybe we'll see you later." I hope not! she told herself. Mary went back inside the palace.

"We've got to get back home now!" Aleesa said to Kenneth. "We don't have any place to go! Do you realize we're stuck in 1893—and without a home?"

"We'll just find the right flower—and maybe if we smell it again, we can get back home," Kenneth said. "Maybe."

Aleesa crossed her fingers for luck. Slowly, they walked back through the gardens. They kept looking at the flowers.

"Is that it?"

"Nah. Look at this one. How about this?"

Finally, Aleesa let out a screech. "Here!" she yelled. She snapped the flower off its stem. Yes! The heavy scent wound around her. She felt dizzy. Everything looked blurry. She handed it to Kenneth before it dropped from her fingers.

Kenneth took a deep sniff of the flower. Sick, he thought. Then his head reeled. He dropped to his knees.

Aleesa's head cleared. She stared at Kenneth.

"Hey!" she almost shouted. "Look!" She grinned.

Kenneth was wearing regular clothes again. She looked down. Yes! The long dress was gone. She was back in jeans and a jacket.

"All right!" Kenneth yelled. He wanted to jump up and down.

"Guess I won't be doing our social studies project in any grass skirt, huh?" Kenneth teased Aleesa. "I didn't see one person in a grass skirt. Or a hut," he added.

"No," Aleesa admitted. "You're right. And now I guess the project won't be *too* bad to work on either," she said. She sighed. "It's really too bad it ended like that. The queen was really special."

"Uh-huh," Kenneth said. "But maybe we can make the class feel the same way we do now. About native rights. We'll think of something."

"Hey!" a voice called. "Hey, you two!" The guard walked around the bend in the path. She frowned. "We've been looking all over the arboretum for you. You're not very responsible. Your teacher, Ms. Harper, has been worried sick. We almost called the rescue squad."

"Nah," Kenneth said. He grinned at Aleesa. "We *are* the rescue squad. You just don't know it!"

And Kenneth and Aleesa gave each other a thumbs-up sign.

Epilogue

Queen Lili'uokalani wrote to U.S. President Grover Cleveland in 1893 after the revolution. She wrote him about the wrongs that had been done to the Kingdom of Hawaii.

President Cleveland sent James Blount to investigate. Blount decided that the revolution was wrong. He called it an "act of war" by the U.S. on Hawaii. President Cleveland then told the provisional government to resign. Cleveland wanted the queen back in power. The provisional government said no, of course. They wanted to keep their power. And the U.S. Congress did nothing.

On July 4, 1894, Sanford Dole announced the formation of the Republic of Hawaii. He was president. Some supporters of the queen revolted. Guns were found. The queen was arrested January 16, 1895, though she was innocent. She was held prisoner in a room in Iolani Palace. This is where she wrote the song "The Queen's Prayer."

Finally, she signed the abdication papers. That meant she agreed she would no longer be queen, ever. In 1896 she was finally set free.

She traveled to Washington, D.C. President Cleveland apologized. But it was too late.

In 1898, Congress voted to annex Hawaii. It became part of the United States. President McKinley wrote, "I am ashamed of the whole affair." Finally, in 1958, Hawaii became a state.

In 1993, the U.S. Congress passed a bill. It was an official apology to the Kingdom of Hawaii. Today, native Hawaiian groups are asking for the same rights that Native Americans have. They would like to have more of a voice in their own affairs. They would like to live Queen Lili'uokalani's dream of a land for her people.

Queen Lili'uokalani

Over a hundred years ago, Hawaii had kings and queens. The native Hawaiians were proud of their royal families. The royalty ruled wisely. They loved their people.

But when foreigners came to the Hawaiian Islands, life changed. First, Christian missionaries came to live. They taught the Christian religion to the Hawaiians. Sadly, they also told the Hawaiians that many of their own customs were wrong and evil. They outlawed the hula for many years.

Then other foreigners came. People came from America, England, Germany, and Italy. They bought or sometimes even took the Hawaiians' land. They made huge sugar cane plantations.

More foreigners came to work on the plantations. Chinese and Japanese flocked to Hawaii to work on the plantations. Foreigners became rich in Hawaii. By the time Queen Lili'uokalani was born, foreigners were a big part of life in Hawaii.

Born into a royal family, Lili'uokalani always knew what it would mean to be royal. She was born September 2, 1838. Then she was adopted by other royal chiefs, Paki and Konia. The Hawaiians' chiefs often adopted each other's children. Raising one another's children was a way of keeping peace. It helped them treat each other with respect. Family and respect were important to Hawaiians and to the royalty.

Lili'uokalani went to the missionaries' Royal School with other royal children. She went to church each Sunday. She was known as intelligent and kind, even when she was small. She spoke and wrote both English and Hawaiian beautifully.

Lili'uokalani loved music. Many people talked about her musical talent. She sang and wrote music. "Aloha Oe" is her most famous song and one dear to Hawaiians' hearts. She married John Owen Dominis, who later became governor of O'ahu, the main island.

Lili'uokalani's older brother became king. King Kalakaua would sometimes go on trips. He traveled to the different Hawaiian islands. He traveled to the United States and all over the world. When he traveled, he often put Lili'uokalani in charge. She ruled Hawaii while he was gone. She learned much about how to rule. It was good practice for the time she would be queen herself. The people loved her. Her personal motto was *Onipu'a*, steadfast, or stubborn. Lili'uokalani was a strong person.

Lili'uokalani was devoted to her Hawaiian people. She liked to help others. She began charities. She helped feed the hungry.

She thought education was important. She began the Lili'uokalani Educational Society to help educate Hawaiian girls. She leased land at good rates to Hawaiians on the island of Hawaii. The money from these rents was put into a special fund for Hawaiians. She also recommended a cut in her income as queen so there would be more money for teachers' salaries. She cared a lot about her people.

Lili'uokalani had a favorite sister, Princess Likelike. Likelike died, but left a daughter, Princess Ka'iulani, who was half English. Ka'iulani became a favorite niece of Lili'uokalani. She went to school in England. Lili'uokalani decided Ka'iulani would be the next queen.

Lili'uokalani traveled also. Because she was royalty, she was treated well. She went to the United States. She visited the White House. President Cleveland welcomed her. She also traveled to England. Queen Victoria of England spent time talking with her and became her friend. Queen Lili'uokalani impressed everyone with her intelligence and grace.

In 1887, foreigners forced King Kalakaua to adopt a new constitution. It was called the "Bayonet Constitution," since he was forced to sign it. This constitution was bad for the Hawaiians. It kept many Hawaiians from voting. It gave the power to the non-Hawaiian foreigners. King Kalakaua died in 1891.

Lili'uokalani became queen in 1891. She faced many problems. Her husband died in the next few months. She missed his wise advice. Many Hawaiians sent her petitions asking her to change the constitution. They wanted their rights back. So she decided to write a new constitution.

But many of the businessmen and sugar planters got angry when the queen said she would have a new constitution. They formed a secret club. It was called the Annexation Club. They wanted to get rid of Queen Lili'uokalani. They wanted all the power. They also wanted to be part of the United States. They thought it would help them.

The Hawaiian sugar plantation owners were losing money. They thought if Hawaii became part of the U.S., they could make money again. The American foreign minister, J. L. Stevens, liked the idea. He wanted Hawaii to be part of the United States too. Some people in the U.S. also wanted to control Hawaii's Pearl Harbor. It was perfect for the U.S. Navy. Mr. Stevens promised the Annexation Club that he would send the U.S. Marines to help them.

Stevens told the queen he would protect her. But he told the Annexation Club a different story.

The queen's ministers betrayed her. They changed their minds about the new constitution. They told her it wasn't a good idea. Queen Lili'uokalani had to back down.

The U.S. Marines landed in Honolulu. Mr. Stevens and the Annexation Club then lied again. They said the marines landed to protect Americans. They said they were afraid of a revolution. But the marines marched to Iolani Palace, the royal palace. They didn't march to Americans' homes to help them. Queen Lili'uokalani and her friends knew the marines were there to overthrow her.

Queen Lili'uokalani was brave. She said she would step down. She decided it would be better to do that instead of starting a war against the U.S. Marines. She knew many of her people would die if that happened. She cared more about her people than about her throne.

Two years later, some Hawaiians began a revolution. They tried to make her queen again. They wanted their rights back. The revolt was put down. Accused of treason, Lili'uokalani was tried and convicted. The court sentenced her to death. But the U.S. protested.

So, instead, she was held prisoner in a room in Iolani Palace for a long time. In that room, she wrote "The Queen's Prayer," a sad and beautiful song. Finally, the new government, run by mostly foreigners and Caucasians, let her go home to Washington Place.

Finally, the U.S. flag flew over Honolulu. The Hawaiian flag was taken down. Hawaii became part of the United States. But the Hawaiians have never forgotten their proud queen who loved them.